She did not remove her clothes, which she often did during an interrogation. It made her feel more at ease and kept her clothes from getting bloody. It also had a psychological effect on the prisoners. With these others in the room, she just put her plastic covering on over her clothes and pulled her tools from the bag she'd brought, spreading them out on the table.

Ariadne picked up the cattle prod. She looked over at Mitch. He was red in the face, shouting at the other men, who were not shy about shouting back. They were still oblivious to her, and to their prisoner.

She wished she had brought some earplugs.

She walked over to the shackled, blindfolded man and watched him quiver. His genitals were shriveled in fear.

She turned on the prod.

This one's for Nick

HARD

BY L. L. SOARES

PART I

CHAPTER 1

He woke to the sound of a woman moaning.

It was soft at first, tugging at the edges of awareness. Then it got louder. And louder.

He rolled over in the bed, wrapped in the sheets, and stared at the window. There were a couple of bananas on the sill that he had put there to ripen. They were starting to rot.

The woman's moans reached a crescendo and then stopped.

He sat there, a mummy of sheets, listening for more.

Nothing.

Merry escaped from his bonds and walked naked to the open window, looking down at the backyard. Or what might be called a backyard. It was really just a vacant lot—some asphalt, long grass, a few discarded bottles. A tiny square of grass.

No one was out there, but from the sound of things, one of his neighbors must have been having a good time.

Merry looked at himself in the mirror beside the bed. He was starting to get a noticeable gut. He was also starting to look old. It didn't sit well with him.

The phone rang.

He'd let the machine get it. It was a Sunday morning, after all. Who got up early on a Sunday, unless you were going to church or something? In his living room, there was still most of a birthday cake on the coffee table. He had gotten it for himself, and he had eaten more of it than he remembered. He was 39 years old. Next year, the 1980s would be over and he would be 40. Where did all the time go? A crushed party hat was on the floor, that and the empty Jack Daniel's bottle beside it were the only other signs that he had celebrated the night before. Not that it was much of a celebration by himself.

He had a slight hangover. If he could have just slept a few more hours, he would have been okay. The ringing phone annoyed him that much more. He felt a sudden desire to answer it anyway. If it was some asshole, it might be fun to give him a piece of his mind. "Hello," he said.

The person didn't answer right away.

"Who is this?"

It was a man's voice, but he didn't recognize it. "I saw you in the window."

"What?" he asked. "Who is this?"

"You've got a real nice dick."

"What?" That didn't make any sense. "Who the fuck is this?"

The man on the other end laughed.

"I hope you had a good look. If I get a hold of you, I'll pop your eyes out for you."

The caller hung up.

"You fucking asshole," Merry grumbled and slammed down the receiver.

Not the best start to a new day. A new *year* alive on the Earth.

He made himself a cup of instant coffee and sat down on the sofa.

He stared at the framed photo on the coffee table. Him and Ariadne. They were laughing, holding each other.

He gave the photo a little push, knocking it to the floor.

This was no time for reminders.

Merry went back into the bedroom and pulled down the shade.

He heard the woman moaning again.

Wrapping himself in a sheet, he gently pulled the shade up a little and glanced down into the yard.

It was coming from the house next door. The first floor.

He wasn't even aware new people had moved in down there. He wasn't sure how he'd like his new neighbors. It was a pleasant enough sound, but it reminded him too much of what was missing in his life.

He got his binoculars out and tried to look into the window, but the shades were drawn. So he looked up instead, and around, trying to peg the guy who'd called him.

He caught some guy across the way, same floor as him, looking at him with binoculars.

"Bastard," Merry said. "I see you."

The man clearly saw that he'd been spotted and pulled down his shade before Merry could get a really good look.

"I'll take care of you," Merry said.

CHAPTER 2

Lilac sat on the front stoop smoking a cigarette. It was a fairly quiet neighborhood, and she was tired from fucking all morning.

Her jet black hair was tied up in a purple ribbon, and she fiddled with it.

A middle-aged guy in cut-off jeans and a Harley Davidson T-shirt walked past her. He looked at her and then looked away.

Looked like the kind of guy who had been athletic once. He had probably been a real looker once, too, but he had started to go to pot. She watched his butt as he walked away down the sidewalk. His butt wasn't half bad for an older guy.

She looked at her watch, wondering if she had enough time to go down to the corner and get herself some orange juice and a donut. She rarely drank coffee; she didn't need it and it was just a habit she never got into. She decided time didn't matter and started strolling up the block.

She wore cut-off jeans as well, but hers were shorter than the middle-aged guy's had been. She'd cut them herself. And she had a big bandana tied around her top. Not that it had to be all that big to cover what she had up there, but it was good enough. Sometimes she thought about getting implants. It would be good for business. But she was deathly afraid of the possibility of weird chemicals leaking inside her, fucking with her insides. Besides, small breasts just accentuated the illusion that she was even younger than she was. That and her baby face. Luckily, *that* was good for business, too.

She ducked into the corner store and sighed when the air conditioning hit her. It was getting warm outside, but not enough for air conditioning yet, and the store had a real chill to it. Inside the bodega, she noticed the guy behind the counter eyeing her as she went up the aisle to the refrigerated section. There were two brands of orange juice. She got the one with the pulp in it.

She took her time going back to the counter, even though goose bumps were starting to rise on her arms. And her nipples must have been visible through the bandana.

There were donuts there under a glass thing.

"Jelly donut," she said.

"You live around here?" the guy asked. He had to be about twenty. Stubble-faced. Not unattractive, but not really her type.

"Just passing through," she said. "How about that donut?"

He got it for her and put it in a bag. He didn't ring the stuff up. It wasn't the first time this had happened.

She got out her money anyway.

"No charge," the guy said. "Put your money away."

She was going to argue but decided it wasn't worth it.

The guy was looking at her like a lonesome puppy, and the musk of her morning work-out probably didn't hurt. She wondered if he smelled it over the cool air.

"Thanks," she said, taking the bag.

"See you when you're *passing through* again," the guy said.

She wasn't in the mood to be too nice. She just grunted and went outside.

It was time she headed back.

She had to be there for her curtain call.

CHAPTER 3

"Open up in there!"

He'd tried knocking first, but there'd been no answer. He heard someone moving around in the apartment. He knew it had to be the right one. It had been easy enough to get one of the other tenants to buzz him in.

They both knew what this was about.

Merry jiggled the doorknob. "Come on, open up."

After a long silence: "I've got a gun."

"Yeah," Merry said. "So what?"

"Leave me alone or you'll be sorry."

"Stop spying on me," Merry said. "Or you're the one who will be sorry."

"I saw you. You've got binoculars. You look at people, too."

"I don't make phone calls and get under people's skin," Merry said. "I don't laugh like some halfwit on the phone."

"Stay away from me."

"You behave, I'll behave," Merry said. "I just wanted to make a point. How easy it is to get in here. Enough of your bullshit."

"I get the message."

"No more phone calls. And I don't want you looking at me anymore."

"You look."

"Just don't let me catch you."

No answer.

Merry moved away from the door and went back downstairs to the street. He looked up and saw the man staring down at him from his window. He couldn't make out what the guy looked like.

He raised his hand and shook his fist, wondering if the guy really did have a gun. "Asshole!" Merry shouted.

He walked back to his building. Along the way, he passed the girl he'd seen on his way up. Then, she had been smoking, sitting on the front steps of the building he'd been sure the moans had come from. He had thought about asking her about it, but didn't want to sound like some nosy creep.

Now she was walking up the street, wearing really short cutoffs and some material tied around her breasts, eating a jelly donut. She had to be about nineteen or twenty. Her long black hair was tied up in a purple ribbon. She was really cute, but probably too young for him to be taking an interest in.

He walked beside her on the sidewalk, tempted to walk faster, just to move past her. He didn't want her to think he was following her. But she caught his eye.

"Hi," she said, smiling. She had some bright red jelly in the corner of her mouth.

"Hello," he said. "Nice morning, isn't it?"

"Pretty warm day," she said.

It was technically spring, but two weeks ago there had still been some snow on the ground. Now it was almost hot out. So much for the seasons.

"Yeah," he said. "Really nice day. Well, see you around," he said. Then he did walk past her, but couldn't resist glancing back at her over his shoulder.

She disappeared up the steps of the house she'd been sitting in front of.

He went back to his place.

He tried to picture her naked, moaning.

It wasn't difficult.

CHAPTER 4

Ariadne was not having a good morning. She'd been hired to get answers, but it was slow going.

She sat on a loveseat drinking a Japanese beer. It would have to do for breakfast. The loveseat and the carpet beneath it were covered with plastic. Even she had on a plastic bib. So much plastic was necessary because of all the blood.

Ariadne looked out the window at the darkening clouds. It was going to rain this afternoon. Her gaze went back to Mr. Fredericks, naked, his arms out at his sides, his hands nailed to the wall.

There was a ball gag in his mouth, but he wasn't trying to speak anyway. He just stared at her.

"I don't have patience for this shit on a Sunday morning," she said.

She took a long pull from the beer bottle. A lot of jobs, she wasn't supposed to leave any marks that might be noticeable. . When she was allowed to cut loose, like this time, it could be quite exhilarating.

But today she just wasn't in the mood.

She finished the bottle, contemplating how she could use it on him, and then went over and yanked down the gag. "Are you ready to end this bullshit?"

He had tears in his eyes and cigarette burns on his cheeks. "Yes," he said softly. His voice was gritty, like sandpaper. All those stifled screams.

"It's about time," Ariadne told him. "You've fucked up my entire morning. And this is supposed to be my day off!"

"I'll tell you whatever you want to know."

"So I won't need the blowtorch?"

"No!" he cried, his eyes opening wider. "No more!"

"Good," she said, standing close. She gently stroked his nose with her index finger. "It's about fucking time."

It was too bad. She had thought of some interesting ways to use the beer bottle on him.

She put the ball gag back in his mouth and went over to the phone. She pushed the right buttons, staring at Fredericks's shriveled cock.

"He's in a cooperative mood now," she said when someone picked up after the first ring. "Come on back."

There was no reply on the other end, just the sound of the phone disconnecting. They were right down the hall and would be here shortly.

She couldn't tell whether Fredericks was staring at her or at nothing at all. He was a broken man. One in a long line of many.

Some people break horses, she thought. I'm a breaker of men.

"You've made quite a mess here," she told him. "Someone's coming. He's the one you'll have to talk to. Don't let me hear you've become uncooperative again, or I'll pick up where I left off."

The man made an odd sound, muffled by the gag.

"I hate to be interrupted when I'm in the shower."

She slipped off the bib and let it drop to the floor, letting him see her naked for a moment. A reward for his change of mind? He was in no condition to be having dirty thoughts, so he probably didn't even notice.

"So nice doing business with you," she said and bowed before she pattered off to the bathroom. After the Japanese beer, the bow just seemed right.

CHAPTER 5

"Where the hell were you?" Tony asked her as she entered the room. "I was just about to shoot around you."

"I got some breakfast," Lilac said, swallowing the last chunk of donut. "Chill out."

"Don't go getting too chummy with the locals," Tony said. "You've got work to do. And we don't need any free advertising about what we're doing here at this point, either."

"The way Chrissie moans, I'm surprised the whole fucking state hasn't heard," Lilac said.

Chrissie was sitting in front of the makeup mirror having her hair touched up. She cleared her throat and said, "I've won awards for that moan. You know, a little enthusiasm wouldn't hurt you, either."

"I do just fine," Lilac said.

"Get with the program," Tony told her. "Get out of those clothes."

Lilac untied the bandana that concealed her chest, setting her B-cups free. *No, I don't need implants,* she thought as she slipped out of her shorts. *I'm perfect just the way I am.*

The makeup lady came over and touched her up. Wiped her mouth.

"Okay, here's the deal," Tony told her. "You're the babysitter. The kid's been asleep for a while. And you're really bored. So you start playing with yourself. The kid's parents come home earlier than expected, and you're real horny. Okay?"

"Sure."

"Let's go for it."

Lilac went over to the couch. She spread her legs wide and

started playing with herself. The cameras were rolling, and she played it to the hilt. She licked her lips hungrily, tasting some jelly left behind by the donut.

Chrissie and a guy named Jack entered from the side.

"Oh my God!" Chrissie cried out. "What are you doing in my house! What if the baby saw you!"

Lilac opened her eyes in mock horror. "Oh no!"

"Just what do you think you're doing, young lady?" Jack asked. He was a once-burly surfer type who'd gotten a little too fat from too much easy living.

Lilac looked at her watch. "You weren't due back for two hours yet!"

"You're an awful girl," Chrissie said, playing the outraged mother the way she moaned—totally over the top.

"And you know what we do to awful girls," Jack said. He unzipped his pants, sporting a healthy helping of hard-on.

Lilac pretended to look shocked, even though she'd seen it a hundred times, and many more that were bigger.

Chrissie went to work on her first, getting down on her knees by the sofa. She had one helluva tongue, and as she worked it, Lilac took Jack into her mouth. She was never a big fan of sucking cock for some reason, but it was part of the job. So she just went through the motions, keeping her eyes closed, trying to enjoy what Chrissie was doing to her, but knowing it wouldn't last.

Sure enough, Chrissie moved away, becoming a solo act as Jack pulled out of her mouth. She leaned back against the sofa, and Jack slipped it into her and start pumping.

Lilac closed her eyes again and gritted her teeth. She kind of sneered, occasionally snorting air. Guys liked that. As Jack fucked her, she tried to think of someone else. *Anyone* else. Sometimes she thought of movie stars—legitimate movie stars—who she thought were cute. Or people she'd met in her straight life who'd be shocked if they knew what she did for a living.

This time she found herself thinking of the middle-aged guy she'd seen outside. She wished she'd been able to have more of a conversation with him, maybe even gotten his name. He looked like he might be twice her age, but she had always had a thing for older men. And he really wasn't in that bad shape.

Thinking of that guy actually got her going, and she abandoned the teeth-gritting thing for some bonafide moans that even gave Chrissie a run for her money. After it was over, she opened her eyes and saw Jack hovering over her, grinning from ear to ear. Like he thought he was the reason she'd had an orgasm.

She looked down at what he'd left all over her belly and sneered at him. She was known for that sneer. It was her trademark.

"Cut!" Tony shouted. "That's a keeper!"

Lilac pushed Jack away and ran to the bathroom to take a long shower.

CHAPTER 6

There was a yelping now. Maybe a different woman. She was having one helluva time.

Merry was stretched out on the bed, and so was the Sunday paper. He had a glass of whiskey in his hand, and he gulped from it now and then. *Hair of the dog*. He kept the shade down even though he was dressed, because he didn't want to be reminded of the peeping tom fucker across the way.

As he listened to the throes of passion from below, he thought of that girl he'd seen outside the building, and he kicked himself for not trying to keep the conversation going. He didn't even get her name. She'd smiled and seemed friendly, and it made him think he might have had a shot with her, but he hadn't even tried. And now, hearing that sound, he thought of her even more. It had been too long since he last got laid.

The phone rang.

He just sat there and drained his glass. Let the machine answer it. It was probably just some telemarketer, anyway.

It rang twice. Three times.

On the fourth ring, the machine would answer it. He got out of bed and went into the living room to refill his glass.

The machine picked it up. After the message, there was a beep. Then a voice spoke. A voice he recognized.

"That bitch moaning giving you a hard-on?"

Merry went over and grabbed the phone. "I thought I told you not to call here, you fucking asshole."

"Did I interrupt you? Did you lose momentum pulling your dick?"

"You sick motherfucker," Merry said. "You'd better hang up

before I come over there and kick your fucking head in!"

"You'd better not come over here again," the man said. "I have a gun, and I'll use it."

"Why the fuck do you keep calling me?" Merry asked. "Does it give you a thrill or something?"

"It's something to do, ain't it?" the man said. "Why don't you open the shade and show me what you got."

"Asshole," Merry said, slamming down the phone.

He turned the volume down to zero on the machine, in case the jerk tried to call back again. He didn't want to deal with him anymore.

Merry refilled his glass and went back to the bedroom to read the paper spread all over the bed. He really needed to pick apart the classifieds. His savings were running low, and he needed to get a job. But he avoided that section for as long as he could, reading everything else first. The phone started ringing again. Ringing and ringing.

The whiskey went down easier and easier.

By the time he got to the classifieds, he couldn't see clearly. Everything was a blur. He brushed all the sections onto the floor and stretched out.

The yelps and moans had stopped long ago. The phone had stopped ringing.

He closed his eyes and tried to go back to sleep.

CHAPTER 7

There was a knock at the door. Ariadne was drying herself off. She grabbed her gun and didn't make a sound. When the knocking persisted, she approached the door.

"What?" she said just loud enough to be heard.

"We're done," came the voice from the other side. "Can I come in?"

"No," she said. "We've discussed this before. When I'm doing a job, I don't mix business and pleasure."

"I just want to talk. Really."

"So talk."

He'd tried to get in before, while she was still in the shower, but she'd locked the door. He could have jimmied it, but that would have meant facing her wrath. It made her feel good he hadn't had the balls.

"Open the door," he said. "Please."

"Wait a minute," she told him, and opened her bag, got out her clean clothes. She took her time putting them on. When she was ready, she opened the door.

He stood there in his slick Italian suit, blocking her way.

"Make it quick," she said.

"You did a great job," he told her. "He was begging to spill his guts."

"That's nice."

"I don't know why you're so mad at me. What'd I do wrong?"

"Nothing, Mitch. It's just that I felt really weird that one time I let you get close after a job. I don't want it to happen again. I want to keep things separate."

"How about we see each other outside this place, when

we're both normal people again?"

"I don't know. Not yet. I have to think about it."

"I wish you wouldn't push me away," he said, grabbing her shoulders. A brave move.

She tensed. "Let me go."

He released her and stepped aside.

She moved past him. "I'm sorry I'm not more fun, but that's too bad."

They walked down the hall to the living room. Fredericks was gone, but the plastic was still there. They were alone.

"My boys took him away," Mitch said. "Like I said, you did a great job."

"That's what you pay me for."

"Yeah." She was wearing an oversized T-shirt and sweat pants. Her wet hair clung to her head like a helmet. The way he was looking at her, she knew that she still looked stunning.

"Clean this place up."

"We always do." He smiled. She knew he had people for that.

He stood there looking at her. "I'll call you. We'll have more jobs for you soon."

She walked toward the door. "Fine," she said, not turning around, her hand on the knob.

"You said you'd think about *us,*" Mitch said. "So think."

She turned the knob and left. She avoided the elevator and took the stairs.

CHAPTER 8

When Merry woke up, it was still daylight. He looked over at the clock. He'd only been asleep about two hours. He got out of bed, stepping on a carpet of newspaper sections.

Right away, he thought of that girl again. The one he'd seen outside. He wanted to see her again. She'd talked to him. She'd seemed interested. Maybe he was reading too much into it and she was just naturally friendly, but he wanted to see her again to be sure.

He left his apartment and walked over to the house where he'd seen her.

She was sitting on the steps, smoking another cigarette, watching him approach.

"Hi," she said, and smiled.

"Hi," he said, feeling stupid.

"I was hoping you'd come by again."

"Really?"

"Sure."

He sat on one of the steps below her. "Are you waiting for someone?"

"Nah, just killing time. They won't let me smoke inside."

"You have friends in there?"

"Kind of," she said. "More like co-workers, I guess."

"You had lunch yet?"

She thought about it. She looked at her watch. "I guess it's about that time, huh?"

"Yeah."

"You live next door?"

"Yep," he said. "But we don't have to eat there."

"You cook?"

"Yeah, sure."

"I haven't had real home cooking in a long time. You any good?"

"Good enough."

"Is that an invitation?"

"Sure, if you want it to be."

She smiled again. "My name's Lilac. For real."

"Mine's Merry."

"Mary?"

"No, Merry. You know, like Merry Christmas. Kind of like being called Happy-you know?"

"Your parents named you that for real?"

"Yeah," he said. "Sounds like we both had imaginative parents."

"I guess so," Lilac said, getting up. He did the same.

"You got any eggs?" she asked. "I know you were talking about lunch, but I could really go for some eggs."

"Yeah, sure. Eggs are okay for lunch. And I have steak."

"Sounds good," she said.

He started moving toward his building. She followed close behind.

"So what kind of work do you do that has you showing up on a Sunday morning?"

"You could say I'm in show biz," she said, and then kind of laughed. "What do you do?"

"I used to be a cop," he said. "But right now I'm unemployed. I just can't decide what to do with what's left of my life. You ever feel like that?"

"All the time," Lilac said.

CHAPTER 9

"So what was it like growing up with a name like Merry?" Lilac asked after chewing a bite of steak. "The kids must have teased you something awful."

"Yeah, it was pretty rough. I got into a lot of fights. But you see, I was good at it. Fighting. So it stopped after a while. How about you?"

"It kind of sucked, too. I didn't have to fight about it, but I remember being really upset about it, wanting to change my name. But I kind of like it now."

"I'm not sure I like Merry any more now than I used to," he said. "I guess I've just grown used to it."

"Thanks for lunch," she said.

"Sure." He put down his utensils. "You want another beer?"

They were sitting in his small kitchen. He went to the refrigerator and pulled out two bottles of beer. "You're old enough to drink, right?"

"I'm twenty-one," Lilac said, sounding annoyed.

"I'm just joking," Merry said. "I really don't give a shit." He twisted the top off one bottle and passed it to her. He twisted the top off his bottle and took a long drink.

"So you live alone, huh?" Lilac asked.

"Yep."

"You ever get lonely?"

"Sure, sometimes.

"Sometimes?"

"Don't you?" He took the plates and put them in the sink.

"You ever been married?" Lilac asked.

"Yeah, sure."

"For how long?"

"About eight years," he said. "It just didn't work out. We got divorced about a year ago."

"What was she like?"

"She was pretty. And at first things seemed pretty good between us. But then, I don't know, she just started drifting away from me. Like she was somewhere else all the time, even though she was right in front of me."

"People change."

"How about you?"

"No, I've never been married."

"Did you ever come close?"

"Not really."

"What's this 'show biz' you mentioned before?"

"I was joking."

"I don't know how to say this, but someone down there was making a lot of noise this morning, woke me up ..."

"That was probably Chrissie. She's pretty loud."

"What is it you *do* down there?"

"You sure you're not a cop anymore?"

"I promise," he said. "I'm so *not* a cop now, it's not funny. I'm not trying to judge you or anything. I'm just curious."

"We're making a movie."

"Oh."

"I don't need to say anymore, huh?"

"I heard enough to know what kind of movie."

"I've been doing that kind of thing for a couple of years now. The money's pretty good, and there's a big market for it."

"Do you like it?" he asked. "I mean, does it bother you at all?"

"No, it doesn't bother me. I can think of a lot worse ways to earn money. Real lousy jobs. You know, I wasn't sure I was going to talk about this. I didn't want to weird you out or anything."

"I kind of already knew. Or, at least it was definitely at the top of my list of guesses."

"I guess you'd have to be deaf not to hear Chrissie. She does get a little carried away. But that doesn't hurt, you know. She's doing real well, in *the business*, you know?"

"I'd think that's a plus in your job."

"Yeah," Lilac said. "They're always telling me to emote more. But that's just not the way I am."

They sat there, drinking beer.

She noticed the half-eaten birthday cake, still in its box, on the coffee table.

"Someone just have a birthday?" she asked.

"Yeah, me."

"How old are you?"

He didn't want to say, then figured *what the fuck.* "Thirty-nine."

"I wouldn't have guessed it."

"Thanks," he said.

"You didn't celebrate by yourself, did you?"

"Yeah, I did."

"That's awful."

"I didn't mind it."

"You should never spend your birthday alone," she said. "Can I have some cake? I'll sing Happy Birthday if you give me some."

"Take what you want," he said. "I'll get some plates."

He cut her a piece of cake, and she started singing, just like she said she would. He sat beside her on the sofa and smiled.

"Thanks a lot," he said, when she was done. "That made up for last night. It was too darn quiet here."

"Thanks for the cake."

"Do you have to be anywhere?" Merry asked.

"No. I've got the rest of the day off. Why?"

"You want to go somewhere? To the park or something?"

"I'm kind of comfortable right here," she said. "Just talking like this is fine. I haven't been able to just talk to someone in a long time. Just hang out. I kind of like it. It's nice to get away from the set."

"Want another beer?" he asked.

"Sure," she said, putting an especially big chunk of cake into her mouth.

CHAPTER 10

Ariadne jogged home and stretched out on her sofa, trying to catch her breath. The phone started ringing.

She picked it up just before the answering machine clicked on. "Yeah?"

"You didn't run all the way home, did you?" Mitch asked.

"Oh, it's you."

"I didn't disturb you, did I?"

"This is my time off. What do you want?"

"Could I interest you in some dinner later? Something real nice? We wouldn't talk shop at all. It'd be a real date."

"You didn't hear a fucking word I said earlier, did you?"

"No need to use such language, Ariadne."

"Don't patronize me," she said. "I'm not a little girl. I don't need daddy's permission."

"I just wanted to show you a good time, help you relax after a hard day's work, that's all. Any harm in that?"

"Look, I told you I wanted to keep this business."

"You said you'd think about it."

"How the fuck can I think about anything if you keep buzzing around me like a horsefly? Just fuck off, okay, Mitch? Don't call me again, unless it's business."

"You know, you should really lighten up."

"Fuck you." She hung up and unplugged the cord. She needed some peaceful time. It was starting to bother her, this thing with Mitch.

In a moment of weakness, they'd had a fling, and she was starting to regret it. She didn't like the idea of someone trying to woo her. It just wasn't what she wanted at this stage in her life.

She preferred to keep things casual.

She just wanted to be *left alone.*

Ariadne climbed out of her sweaty clothes and sat down again on the sofa.

She closed her eyes and tried to purge her mind. Instead, she got a cavalcade of images. Mr. Fredericks begging for mercy. Mitch breathing hard as he fucked her. And she even thought of Merry. Christ, she hadn't thought about him in months. She wondered what he was doing right now.

Sometimes she regretted their breakup. There had been plenty of good things about their marriage, but those cop instincts ... that goddamned curiosity of his. It'd ruined everything.

Ariadne sat up. She was never going to get any rest at this rate.

She leaned over and got the bottle of sleeping pills from her night table. She went into the bathroom to get a cup of water. She stared at herself in the mirror.

Am I getting too old for this shit? she wondered.

It was kind of early to go sleep, but she had been up for almost 24 hours by now. She thought the run would tire her out, but she was still wide awake. Sometimes it got like this. She couldn't turn the engine off. Sometimes she needed help.

She popped three pills and washed them down with tap water.

CHAPTER 11

They hadn't planned on it, either of them, but here they were on the living room carpet, fucking each other's brains out.

Lilac didn't want to seem like a slut, despite what she did for a living. She wanted to take it slow, nurture it. But something about him, about the way he was so down-to-earth, the way he made her feel so comfortable, just broke her willpower. Besides, who knew how much longer she would be here?

They both wanted it, she knew, even though they'd both resisted. Both tried to play it cool.

And now here they were, fucking like wild dogs.

They hadn't even made it to the bedroom. The carpet was burning Lilac's back as she was dragged against it. Her cutoff jeans were somewhere on the other side of the room. Her bandana was tied around Merry's head.

She didn't remember who had made the first move. It had just been so fluid.

She gritted her teeth, hissing breath, and then she just lost it, unaware of what she was doing, getting totally swept up in the moment.

He was kissing her, fucking her.

He came and still kept pumping away as long as he could.

They had been rolling around on the carpet, banging into furniture and knocking things over. They had been oblivious to everything but each other.

When they stopped, exhausted and drenched in sweat, they held each other for a while and tried to catch their breaths.

"That was wild," Lilac said, breathing like an asthmatic in his arms.

"Do you think I have a future in show biz?" he asked.

"Forget show biz, honey. I want you all to myself."

"But we just met," he said, and laughed.

"Just shut up," she said, smirking.

"Hey, how about another beer?" He moved, and she squeezed him tighter, not letting him go.

"Let's just stay like this for a while, okay?"

She heard him say "Okay," softly above her. She had her head pressed against his chest and could hear his heartbeat as well.

The phone rang.

Lilac felt him tense up. His heart beat a little faster.

"Ignore it," she pleaded.

Second ring.

"I hate the outside world," Lilac said. "Why can't it all just disappear?"

Third ring.

"Don't worry," Merry said. "I'm not going anywhere."

Fourth ring.

They sat there, wrapped up in each other, intent on not moving, both listening for the machine to pick it up. Waiting to find out who was calling. Who dared invade their sanctuary?

"Can you keep the noise down?" a man's voice said. "Do you have to let the whole world know you're finally getting fucked?"

"That cocksucking son of a bitch," Merry said, gently pushing her aside and charging for the phone. But the caller had already hung up.

"Who was that?"

"Some voyeur fuck who lives across the way," Merry said, glaring at the phone. He knew he shouldn't have turned the machine's volume up again.

"I swear I'm going to kill that motherfucker one of these days."

CHAPTER 12

BZZZZZZZZZZZZZZZZ.
Ariadne reluctantly woke to the sound of the door buzzer.

"Shit, I should have disconnected that too," she muttered, getting to her feet.

With all the shades down, it was dark in the room, but the glow-in-the-dark numbers of her clock radio told her it was almost seven p.m. She was still groggy as she got up and walked to the hallway outside her bedroom door, where the intercom box was. She pressed the button and asked, "Who is it?"

"Francie."

She buzzed her in and went back to the bedroom to throw on her clothes, feeling like there was gauze inside her head and hoping it would dissolve soon.

By the time Francie made it upstairs and knocked on her door, Ariadne was ready for her.

"Did I just wake you?" Francie asked

"Don't worry about it," Ariadne said. "I got enough sleep."

"I tried to call first, but you wouldn't answer your phone."

"It's disconnected. I didn't want to be disturbed. You want a drink?"

"You got any wine?"

"Sure." Ariadne went to the kitchen and got out an unopened, chilled bottle and removed the cork.

"I haven't seen you in a while, so I thought I'd drop by," Francie said. She was an attractive black woman in her early thirties. She and Ariadne had known each other since they were teenagers.

Ariadne would probably have been pissed off at anyone else who woke her from a sound sleep. But she would forgive Francie just about anything.

"So how's it going?"

Francie took a sip. "Okay. Would you be interested in going to a movie? There's a real good one down at the art theater."

"I don't know how social I feel right now," Ariadne said. "I had to work earlier this morning."

"Oh."

"What does that mean?"

"Nothing."

"You say 'oh' like it's a death sentence."

"Have you changed your line of work?"

"No."

"Well, I guess it bothers me, that's all."

"Tough."

"I've known you a long time," Francie said. "And I still don't get it. You were the nicest, most well-adjusted girl I knew growing up, and now you get your kicks making people scream."

"I never said I get my kicks from it," Ariadne said.

"Bullshit. If it bothered you, you wouldn't do it."

"It's just a job, that's all."

"Whatever."

"It doesn't bother me. That doesn't mean it gets me off."

"How did you ever get caught up in all that, anyway?"

"Dad worked for the government. I got interested in torture. He made sure I was taught by the best. And now I have a profession."

"Shit."

"I have the stomach for it. I'm good at it. It's just a job, Francie. It pays the rent."

"I still think it's fucked up."

"Let's change the subject, okay?"

Francie took a long drink, draining the glass. "Got any more?"

"Of course I do," Ariadne said, pouring her a refill. "You've never mentioned what I do to anyone else, have you?"

"Of course not. I wouldn't know how to."

"I know you, Francie, you get off on shocking people."

"You swore me to secrecy long ago. I stay sworn."

"I had to tell someone," Ariadne said. "Or I would have gone nuts. Heaven knows I couldn't tell Merry when we were married. You should have seen him when he found out. Like someone had hit him with a sledgehammer. He couldn't believe it."

"I sympathize."

"The difference is, he took off like a shot when he found out. You've stuck by me."

"I try not to think about it too much."

"You don't have to think about it at all."

"To think things like that still go on in the world. It sounds so medieval. I mean, you might not be surprised to hear about it happening in some third-world country, but right here, in the same city we live in? It scares the shit out of me."

"Why should it? It might be in the same city, but it's not the same world. It's a world you'll never come into contact with."

"I sure hope not."

"I like that aspect. When I leave it, I can escape into the real world. Just leave it all behind."

"You have to admit, there has to be this kind of psycho part of your personality to be able to do this."

"I don't know if *psycho* is the right word, but, yes, I do have a dark side, and this lets me indulge it in a totally legal way. Plus, I get paid good money. Do you ever think that a surgeon must have the same kind of impulse, in order to be able to cut someone open in the first place? Think of me like a kind of a surgeon."

"I don't think it's the same thing at all," Francie said. "A surgeon *heals* people. Let's change the subject."

"You're the one who brought it up."

"You sure you don't want to go to the movies? Get out of this place for a while?"

"Maybe."

"So anything happening on the guy front?"

"No, not really," Ariadne said. "Some fuck from work keeps

trying to get together with me, but I keep blowing him off."

"Kind of ruins the idea of separate worlds, huh?"

"Yeah," Ariadne said. "I guess he's okay. We had a little fun, but that's it. Now he's gone all soft and puppy dog on me, and I don't have the stomach for it."

"Is it because he has something to do with your work, or is it that you don't want a serious relationship just yet?"

"A little of both, probably," Ariadne said. Then, "Actually, a *lot* of both. I just don't need the baggage right now. And he actually had the balls to call me at home and ask me on a real date. That really got me going."

"Let him know it's over."

"I tried. I don't know, maybe I *am* attracted to him. But I don't want a boyfriend. I like living alone, having my space. I've always been that way, Francie. If anyone knows that, you do."

"I know. I'm surprised you and Merry lasted so long."

"Me too. I have to admit, he was something special when we first met. It didn't hurt that we kept completely different hours, because of our jobs, too. It kept us out of each other's hair."

"So do you ever hear from him?"

"No. He's out of my life for good. I even heard he quit the force. He's dropped out completely. I don't even know if he's in the same state anymore. He might have packed up and headed to the west coast for all I know. He always said he wanted to do that."

"Look," Francie said. "It sounds like you really need a break from everything. Come on, let's go somewhere. Get lost in a movie."

"I'd like to."

"Then what's holding you back? Are you waiting for that guy from work to call again or something?"

"I unplugged the phone, remember?" Ariadne said. "He can't bother me unless I let him."

"You really have to resolve this."

"I know. I hate being in this position. Maybe I should just take a vow of celibacy. That would solve everything."

"And have you go even more nuts than normal? No thanks," Francie said. "If anything, you need to get laid *more* often."

Ariadne smirked at her. "I sound like an idiot, don't I?"

"No," Francie said. "You just sound confused, that's all. Like maybe this guy gets to you. It's a change from the Ariadne who charges through life, not taking any shit. It might even be a pleasant change."

"Hold your tongue."

"Do you know how long it's been since I've seen you laugh? My god, you can be a drag sometimes. I don't know why I put up with you."

"Because you're the only person who can."

"Well, you'd better hope that never changes. You try even *my* patience sometimes."

"Okay, okay," Ariadne said. "Let's go to that movie."

CHAPTER 13

"What's with the key?" Lilac asked.

They were on Merry's bed, just holding each other, listening to the whirring of the fan.

"Huh?" Merry said, lost in thought.

"The one around your neck?"

He absently touched it, like he had never noticed it before. It was a thick, bronze-colored key hanging from a shoelace around his neck.

"I don't know," he said. "Just something I picked up."

"How do you *just pick up* something like that?"

"I found it when I was a kid. I thought it was lucky or something. Back then, I used to think it would open something important, like a treasure chest or something. Fate brought it to me, and fate would lead me to what it opened."

"How long ago was that?"

"I don't know, maybe I was eleven, twelve."

"You must have been a silly kid."

"I used to wear my house key around my neck when I was a kid. Sometimes I'd lose it if it was in my pocket, so my mother made me wear it so I couldn't lose it. I was always losing things, I guess. When I found this other key out on the sidewalk one day, I put that around my neck, too. And it's been there ever since."

"Why would you still wear it after all these years?"

"Because I haven't found what it opens yet."

"So you're *still* silly."

"I guess."

"You don't really think it opens anything, do you?"

"Probably not any lock I'll ever come across. Probably some other kid lost his house key, and I found it. Only it doesn't look like a house key, does it?"

She examined it. It was thick, oddly shaped.

"No, I guess not. What did your wife think about it?"

"She thought it was strange, maybe. We didn't talk about it much. After a while, she probably just didn't notice it anymore. Toward the end, we didn't talk about much of anything."

"Do you want to come with me to work tomorrow?"

"I thought you said you were done."

"I just have one more scene. I think you'll like it. Just me and Chrissie."

"I don't know," Merry said. "Do they allow strangers on the set?"

"I'll square it," Lilac said. Then, "Look, you don't have to come if you don't want to. I just thought you might be curious to see what it's like, that's all."

"Let me think about it, okay?"

"Yeah, sure."

He hugged her closer. "You hungry?"

It was starting to get dark outside.

"Can we have something delivered?" Lilac asked. "I don't really want to go anywhere."

"Aren't you the homebody," Merry said. "Well, there's a Chinese place nearby that delivers. I have a menu around someplace. They have great Szechuan."

"Sounds good."

He went to get up, but she had her arms around his middle, and she squeezed him again. "No rush," she said. "Let's just stay like this a little while longer, okay?"

CHAPTER 14

The movie let out late. It was a light, Italian comedy with sub-titles, and Ariadne might have enjoyed it if she hadn't fallen asleep about half an hour into it.

When it was over, they walked through the park. It was a nice night for it.

"You didn't ask me what I thought of the movie," Ariadne said, and laughed.

"You didn't miss much," Francie said.

"Why didn't you nudge me?"

"It wasn't as good as I thought it would be. Besides, you looked so peaceful, and I thought you probably needed the rest. And you don't snore."

"Lucky thing, huh?"

"It's a beautiful night."

"Yeah," Ariadne said, staring at the stars.

"I'm glad you came with me."

"Well, I didn't want you to have to go alone."

"Want to go for a drink?"

"Can we just head back to my place?" Ariadne asked.

"Okay, if that's what you want."

"I'm just not in the mood to be around people. In a movie theater, no one bothers you, but a bar's different."

"Sure."

They hailed a cab and went back to Ariadne's apartment.

Back at the apartment they opened another bottle of wine and watched television. Ariadne fell asleep again. Francie got her undressed and somehow got her to bed.

Ariadne woke up in the middle of the night to the hum of the air conditioner. Francie was gone.

She wished she hadn't.

CHAPTER 15

Merry was wading through blood, vines, and cobwebs, brushing his face as he tried to find the way out. He couldn't tell where he was, whether it was a room or if he was outside. The sky was black. But the blood, a lake of blood he was wading through, was bright neon red. Glowing.

He couldn't feel the blood. His submerged feet were numb.

Up ahead someone was screaming, and even though it went against his instincts, and against all logic, he moved toward the voice because it was a sign of life in an otherwise lifeless void.

The blood got deeper as he advanced. Deeper and thicker. It took more and more effort to slog through it.

Shadows became blurred images.

There were two people. One person's hands were above its head, chained to a wall. The other person was cutting into the chained one with something.

At first Merry couldn't even make out what sex they were.

Then it became clear they were women. One was chained up, screaming. The other was going to town on her with a straight razor, cutting deep grooves into her sides and breasts.

Their faces were obscured by shadows, but their eyes glowed neon red, like the blood. The chained woman struggled and writhed, screaming on and on. The torturer stared at him and hissed like a gorgon. He got close enough to see her face.

It was Ariadne.

The other woman's face was becoming clearer too, but before he could see it, he opened his eyes and sat up in bed.

Two fans whirred away in the dark. Lilac lay huddled asleep in a ball beside him. He was breathing hard. Almost as hard as he had when he was an asthmatic kid. He thought he'd outgrown it, but now he wasn't sure. He didn't have an inhaler handy, but his breath slowly became normal again.

Lilac slept through it. His noises didn't wake her.

He got his breathing under control and got out of bed.

He walked slowly down the hall, feeling the walls as he went along. When he got to the kitchen, he turned the light on.

The dream lingered, as if it had almost become reality and his waking had just barely prevented it.

He opened the refrigerator and hesitated. He reached for a beer, but he was dehydrated, and he knew it would only make him worse. He grabbed a jug of orange juice and drank right from the container until he wasn't thirsty anymore. Then he put it back and shut off the lights.

He moved around in the dark feeling his way down the hall. He slid into bed beside Lilac and wrapped his arms around her. He could barely hear her breathing, unless he pressed his ear to her back. She was so soft.

She stirred gently, but didn't wake.

He held on to her until he drifted back to sleep.

CHAPTER 16

Ariadne woke again, a little later in the night. She turned on the light. She was naked and cold. She got out of bed, turned off the air conditioner, and went out to the living room.

She thought about calling Francie to apologize for falling asleep again, but she was probably sleeping by now herself, and waking her wouldn't help anything.

Ariadne picked up the receiver and thought about who she wanted to call. She wanted to talk to someone. Her fingers pressed 411-for Information.

The operator answered. Ariadne hesitated and then gave the name of the city and Merry's name. Ariadne wrote the number on a pad she kept by the phone.

Merry still lived in the city. Not the greatest neighborhood—he'd definitely gone down in the world-but he hadn't yet taken off for parts unknown. He was accessible. And she wanted to talk to someone.

She picked up the receiver again and pressed his numbers.

It rang a few times and then went to the answering machine.

Ariadne put the phone down. There was no reason to leave a message. If Merry wanted to talk to her, he would have made the effort by now. Obviously, he had gone on with his life. Just like she had.

And there was something to be said for that.

She decided not to bother him. It was a dumb idea. It wasn't like her to move backwards anyway.

She thought about Mitch. But that was a dead end. She didn't want to encourage him, give him false hope. There was no one else she wanted to call. It was too late to bother anyone, and she really didn't have anything to say anyway. It was just an irrational need to reach out. An urge. A desire for human contact. It happened sometimes, *even to her.*

CHAPTER 17

"Are you sure about this?" Merry asked. "I mean, you can change your mind and tell me to forget about it."

"No," Lilac said. "I want you to see firsthand what I do for a living. I want you to know, so there aren't any mysteries."

"You know, you've been very honest with me," he said. "There's no question about that. You don't have to go this far."

"But I *want* to."

"We just met. You don't owe me anything."

"But it feels like we've known each other forever," she told him. "The way we can talk to each other. The way it felt being together. It's uncanny."

He had to agree there. Everything was happening so fast, Merry wasn't sure what to make of it all.

"I don't want to make any problems for you."

"It's the last day of shooting," Lilac said. "Most of it's in the can. Nobody will mind. Will you just relax already?"

"Okay."

It had been a pleasant morning so far. When Merry woke, Lilac was already up. She'd showered and dressed and had even made him breakfast. French toast. He hadn't had that in years. She'd gone out for maple syrup, or whatever that stuff was made of. It was too cheap to be *real* maple.

They walked up the steps to the apartment house where Lilac had been working, the same building he'd passed so innocently the day before, not fully realizing what was happening within—though the moans emanating from there the previous morning had certainly been a dead giveaway, now that he thought about it.

Lilac rang the intercom. Someone buzzed them in.

The apartment was on the ground floor and the door was open.

The place was in chaos. Light stands and cameras on tripods were everywhere, and underwear lay scattered across the floor. Empty food containers and cups that had once held soda or coffee were randomly scattered throughout the room.

In one room, a bleach-blonde, who looked to be anywhere from her late-twenties to her late-thirties was putting on makeup. She was dressed in a bra and panties, staring in a mirror propped against the wall. Merry assumed this was Chrissie. She was attractive, but there were little wrinkles around her eyes, and there was some flab on her belly. Not enough to be a turn-off, though.

Merry kind of liked it.

"Who's this guy?" a man asked.

Merry whirled around and saw Lilac standing beside a guy with dark hair that was graying around the edges, and a matching mustache. He assumed this was Tony.

"Hi," Merry said, not so sure what he was doing here, after all.

"He's with me," Lilac said. "I wanted him to see where I worked."

"Are you kidding me?" Tony asked her. "This isn't Disneyland, baby, and I don't like tourists on my set."

"He's okay," Lilac said. "Really he is. Besides, I wanted him to see my scene with Chrissie. I think it will turn him on."

"Listen, I don't want to be a problem," Merry said. "If you want me to leave, I'll leave."

"He won't be any trouble," Lilac said, pleading. "Let him stay, okay?"

"Well," Tony said, looking Merry over. "It's the last day, and there's not much left to do. If he wants to stay, he can. But stay the fuck out of my way while I'm working. And keep quiet, okay? I don't need any audience participation."

"Fine," Merry said. "You won't even know I'm here."

"Come with me," Lilac said, grabbing his hand and leading him into another room. It was pretty bare. Some dresses hung in a closet. A couple of chairs. And a tall mirror was propped against a wall.

"So this is what they mean by low-budget, huh?"

"Yep," Lilac said. "It's not Hollywood, that's for sure. But they put out a good product, and it does make money."

She turned on the light and started digging into a bag on the floor for lipstick and powder.

"You have to do your own makeup, too?"

"Sometimes somebody comes by to do touch-ups, but we basically do most of it ourselves. It's not that tough." She pulled a chair over to the mirror and sat down.

"You sure I'm not in the way here?"

"Would I have brought you here if I thought you'd be in the way?"

"I don't know." He stood there watching her get ready.

There was a knock at the door.

"Come in," Lilac said, as she applied lipstick.

"I just wanted to say, hi," another guy said as he entered the room.

Merry could tell that Lilac wasn't all that eager to have company. It was obvious that this guy made her uncomfortable.

"What are you doing here, Jack?" she asked. "You're not in any of today's scenes."

"What, don't you like seeing me?"

Lilac made a face.

"Jack?" Merry asked. "Jack Underwood?"

"Merry? I thought it was you when you walked in, but I wasn't sure."

They looked each other over.

"Man, it's been a long time," Merry said. "I haven't seen you since high school!"

"Well, I moved out West, and then I decided to come back. I didn't want to hog the sun all to myself, you know?"

They both laughed.

Merry felt a little tense, even though he was laughing. Back in high school, he'd been a quiet, skinny kid. Jack was one of the guys who'd treated him like shit. A real loudmouth bully type. Merry had wanted to beat the shit out of him for years but hadn't had the guts or confidence to do it. Jack had been bigger, more athletic, and certainly more popular. Now time had changed them both. Merry was bigger than him now, taller and beefier. Jack looked worn out, tired, like a middle-aged beach bum. But there wasn't any reason to kick Jack's ass anymore. Time had made that irrelevant. The laughter they shared now was like Jack's attempt at a peace offering.

They shook hands and continued laughing, even though the joke really hadn't been all that funny, hadn't even been much of a joke at all.

"So what did you do out West?" Merry asked.

"A little bit of everything. I got a football scholarship to UCLA, but I got injured pretty early on. After college, I just stayed out there for a couple of decades. Going pro wasn't in the cards for me, so I tried to break into the movie business. That just didn't work out either. So I kicked around, doing a lot of surfing, taking a lot of odd jobs. I even did stunt work for a while. And then I got into *this* business. I'm making more money now than I ever did, and I get all the pussy I can eat."

He grinned over in Lilac's direction. She ignored him, working on her face. Merry didn't know how to react to that crack, so he let it pass. This wasn't his world. He didn't know the rules.

"So what have you been doing with your life?" Jack asked.

"This and that," Merry said. "Kicking around, you know? I was a cop for about eight years, but I got out of that. It didn't suit me." Merry looked back on his life. It had consisted of a lot of mistakes and a lot of wasted time.

"A cop, huh? I hope you didn't come here to bust us?" Jack said and then laughed. "This isn't a set-up, is it, Lilac?"

"I'm not a cop anymore," Merry said, regretting he'd said anything at all. "And I don't have any problem with what you guys are doing."

"So what brings you here, Merry boy?"

"He's my guest, if you don't mind," Lilac said, turning to face him. "What the fuck are you doing here today anyway?"

"I came to talk to Tony about some money," Jack said, his mouth almost a sneer.

"Well, Tony's in the *other* room," Lilac said.

"I'm just being sociable," Jack said. "I wanted to say hello to my co-star. It's funny, but I thought you liked me a lot better yesterday."

"Well, I guess I'm just a moody cunt," Lilac said. "Do you mind? I'm trying to get ready for my scene."

"Not very friendly today, is she?" Jack asked Merry. "You should have seen her yesterday, during shooting. She couldn't get enough of me."

"It's called *acting*," Lilac said to her reflection.

Merry was starting to realize that, despite the passage of time, he still wanted to kick Jack's ass.

"Get the fuck out, okay?" Lilac said.

"What a mouth on you," Jack said, and then laughed at his own little innuendo.

"See you around, huh?" Merry said, trying to get rid of him.

"Yeah, sure," Jack said. "Maybe we'll have drinks sometime, talk about the old days. Man, those high school days, what a ton of laughs. You remember those days, don't you, Merry?"

Of course he did. They were burned into his brain. All that pent-up anger. The old feelings were starting to resurface.

"You bet," Merry said, forcing a smile that he knew came out grotesque, but by this time he didn't care.

"You thinking of joining the business?" Jack asked. "It's a lot of fun. You get to fuck all kinds of chicks. Nice young ones. Hot older ones. All horny as hell."

"Can't you take a hint?" Lilac shouted.

"Okay, okay," Jack said. "I was just chewing the fat with an old friend, that's all. You're the one who brought him here."

"See you," Merry said.

Jack smiled at Merry and opened the door to leave.

"There you are," Tony said, standing near the doorway.

"Yeah, here are I am."

"So where have you been living these days?" Tony asked. "We miss you back in Cali."

"Believe it or not, I grew up around here," Jack said. "My father died not too long ago, and I've got to get my parents' house ready to sell at some point, so I've been staying there."

Tony looked in at Merry and Lilac. "Excuse us, won't you?"

"Jack was just leaving, anyway," Lilac said.

"Come with me," Tony said to Jack. "I wanted to get your opinion about this shot."

As they walked away, Merry closed the door.

"Were you really friends with that guy in high school?" Lilac asked, taking her clothes off. She went over to the closet to choose something else.

"Not really," Merry said. "He was kind of a jock asshole back then."

"He hasn't changed then."

"We just knew each other, that's all."

Lilac laughed. "For a minute there I thought I'd made a mistake. I don't know if I could really fall for a guy who was buddies with that jerkoff."

Merry laughed. "I hated him in school. I always wanted to beat the shit out of him."

"Why didn't you?"

"I didn't have the balls then," Merry said. He answered honestly, but he wished he hadn't. He didn't like sounding vulnerable. "Besides, he always had a bunch of buddies around him to back him up."

"That's okay," Lilac said. "I know you could do it now, if you wanted to."

"Probably."

"He was all proud of himself yesterday. He really thought he did me a favor."

"So you had sex with him?"

"Of course. He's a male lead. That's one of the drawbacks about this job. Having to get close to shitheads like that. If you kind of distance yourself, it isn't too bad, though. I like to think of someone else. So, like I was saying, he really thought he got me off yesterday. But it wasn't him at all. I was thinking of *you* the whole time."

"You were?"

"Yeah, I'd seen you outside, and I thought you were cute. See, I liked you right away."

He felt uneasy thinking of her fucking that bastard, but he

knew she was trying to ease his mind.

"Thanks," he said, not knowing what else to say.

"You ready in here?" Tony said, sticking his head in. "We're ready for you now."

"Okay," Lilac said, putting on a Catholic schoolgirl uniform.

CHAPTER 18

Ariadne was in the living room lifting dumbbells, watching a sleazy talk show—the topic was parents who lusted after their children's friends.

Ariadne put down her weights and answered her ringing phone.

"It's Mitch. I have another job for you."

"When?"

"Tonight. Midnight."

Ariadne thought about it. She didn't like to work that late, but hers wasn't the kind of job that had banker's hours. The pause must have made Mitch nervous, because he felt a need to fill the space. "I'm sorry it's so late, but things won't be ready until then."

"No problem, I'll be there. Now, where's 'there'?"

"Same place as before," Mitch said. "It's clean and ready for more."

"We haven't used the same place twice in a long time," Ariadne said.

"Well, we're doing it tonight. It's kind of short notice, and it's the best I can do."

"Okay, okay," Ariadne said. "It doesn't matter to me."

"I know it's kind of soon, with the last job just yesterday and all, but this is kind of an emergency. And you know how good you are."

"Thanks," Ariadne said softly, trying not to sound annoyed. It was her job, after all. And it wasn't *his* fault. She'd been kind of tense today, anyway. Maybe she could burn off some of this nervous energy interrogating someone. "Don't worry about it."

"Good," Mitch said.

"I don't mind. And I can always use the money."

"See you then."

"Yeah," Ariadne said, and hung up. She thought about Mitch, wondering if there was any chance at all she'd want to pursue things with him. There were too many complications. If anything went wrong, it could make her job very uncomfortable.

But it had been a long time since she'd really pursued anyone.

She'd have to think about it a while longer. It wasn't something she could decide overnight.

Ariadne went back into the living room and grabbed the dumbbells. There was a commercial for detergent on.

"It gets all kinds of stains out. Grass stains. Even blood," the announcer's voice said.

"I'll have to pick some of that up," Ariadne said.

CHAPTER 19

Lilac was sitting on a bed, looking down at her shoes.

Chrissie was waiting for her cue to enter.

"Wait a minute," Tony said. He looked over at Merry.

"You got a minute there, pal?"

"Sure," Merry said.

Tony led him into one of the spare rooms.

"Is there some kind of problem with me being here?" Merry asked when they were out of earshot.

"That's up to you," Tony said. "Jack said something to me about you being a cop."

"I used to be," Merry said. "But I'm not anymore. Haven't been for a while."

"You being straight with me?"

"Yeah," Merry said. "Hey, I didn't come here to make any problems for you. If you want, I'll just leave."

"Normally I don't care," Tony said, "if one of the girls wants to bring a boyfriend or something on the set. Sometimes I even get new blood that way. It's just that I have to watch my ass, you know?"

"I know."

"I know Lilac, she usually has pretty good instincts about people. Jack, he don't know shit. So I'm going to trust you on this. Besides, you know enough already to bust my balls if you were still on the force."

"I'm not," Merry said. "I don't have a problem with any of this."

"Okay, you can stay," Tony said. "Just keep it quiet, okay? I want to get this done today."

"Sure."

"By the way, you interested in a job?" Tony asked.

"I'm not sure."

"Think about it. You're not half bad. And sometimes the girls really give it their all if they like a guy."

"I'll think about it."

"Good," Tony said. "Now I have to get back to work."

Tony went back to the living room, where the bed had been set up. Lilac smiled at Merry. Chrissie looked impatient, waiting for her cue.

"Action," Tony said.

Chrissie entered the room. She stood next to the bed.

"What are you doing in my bedroom?" Chrissie asked. "I thought you went home."

"I was waiting for you, Mrs. Crabtree."

"Were you?"

"Yes, Mrs. Crabtree," Lilac said, trying to look as innocent as possible. The outfit she wore actually made her look younger. "I wanted to talk to you alone about my grades."

Merry was standing off to the side, and the bathroom door opened behind him. Someone walked by and tapped him on the shoulder.

Turning, Merry saw that it was Jack. He grinned at Merry and gave him a thumb's up. Then he left. Merry just stared at the door where Jack had been. *I just know I'm going to have to kick his ass at some point*, Merry thought.

Turning back to the action, Merry saw that Chrissie and Lilac were undressing one another, kissing as they did so.

"It's so nice to have you all to myself, Mrs. Crabtree," Lilac said.

"I feel the same way, Sissy," Chrissie said, pressing Lilac down on the bed with her body. "I want to show you just how much I appreciate all the effort you've been putting into your studies."

Chrissie spread Lilac's legs and went down on her. Lilac was propped up against pillows, licking her lips and breathing heavy. Even through her half-closed eyes Merry could tell she was looking at him.

His cock got hard and he was almost embarrassed, but no one was interested in him. The cameraman, the small crew, Tony—they were all focused on the action.

Lilac started moaning, and Merry knew it was for him. All for him.

CHAPTER 20

By the time Ariadne got to the hotel room, she was almost late, which was not like her at all. The room was already prepared for her, with plastic sheeting spread around the subject who was shackled to the wall, naked and shivering beneath his blindfold. She didn't have to ask whether the room was soundproofed.

Despite the preparations, she found chaos awaiting her as well. Several men in suits paced around the room, shouting at one another. Mitch stood in a corner, trying to sink into the wall when she first walked in. Soon afterwards, he had moved forward and was joining in on the shouting.

There was a problem. Someone had made a mistake. They were blaming each other. That much she understood.

None of their shouts were directed at her. In fact, they did not even seem to notice her. She put her bag down on a nearby table and turned to face them. While they continued to ignore her, she wondered what she was doing here. Weren't there other ways to make a living? Maybe Francie was right and she secretly did get off on it.

As soon as she had entered the building she knew something was wrong. Security was extra tight. She'd had to pass two checkpoints—by-the-book bastards she'd never seen before, who seemed amused and more than a little annoyed that a woman was doing a job they clearly thought only men had the stomach for.

She stood there, trying to block out the shouting men, but staring at them just the same.

And then Mitch walked over to her.

"Can you start on him right away?" Mitch asked, pointing to the guy who was shackled. "I have to sort some things out here."

"Will you be leaving me alone with him?"

"Not this time," Mitch said. "We'll be questioning him while you work your magic. No time for you to soften him up. Just dive right in."

Usually she worked until the subject was dying to talk, and then the others came in. It reduced any distractions, and let her focus on her work.

She did not remove her clothes, which she often did during an interrogation. It made her feel more at ease and kept her clothes from getting bloody. It also had a psychological effect on the prisoners. With these others in the room, she just put her plastic covering on over her clothes and pulled her tools from the bag she'd brought, spreading them out on the table.

Ariadne picked up the cattle prod. She looked over at Mitch. He was red in the face, shouting at the other men, who were not shy about shouting back. They were still oblivious to her, and to their prisoner.

She wished she had brought some earplugs.

She walked over to the shackled, blindfolded man and watched him quiver. His genitals were shriveled in fear.

She turned on the prod.

He was completely tense, like a guitar string pulled too tight. As though he could sense her there, in front him. She didn't have to touch him to know that.

At first, she zapped him randomly. He had no idea where the pain would come from next, since he couldn't see her. He just writhed, trying to protect himself. But it was futile.

When she shocked his testicles, the noise he made drew the attention of the others. They stopped arguing, she noticed as the room finally grew quiet.

They moved over to where she was.

She had her back to them and pretended not to notice.

Mitch stepped forward and removed the gag, then stepped back.

They barked questions at the man in a language she didn't

recognize, as Ariadne continued working. Every once in a while, she stopped to give him a chance to reply, and would then go back to what she was doing.

She was done playing around with the cattle prod. There were other tools to employ. Ariadne liked variety. Some were power tools that vibrated in her hands. Others were more primitive and needed more involvement. She took her time trying them out.

All the while, the men shouted their questions. The prisoner began to answer. She slowed but didn't stop. When there were silences that lasted too long, she started applying pain again.

She stayed away from the prisoner's genitals for at least an hour before she picked up the vice grips. That seemed to do the trick. He found his tongue and the answers carne fast and furious. She didn't understand a lot of what they were talking about, and she didn't care. There was a time when it interested her, but now she was more focused on inflicting pain.

Mitch touched her shoulder. She stepped back and watched the shouting men.

"Am I done already?" she asked.

"We got what we wanted," he said. "You can leave now if you want."

He left her and went back to the others.

Ariadne stood by the table, looking down at the tools of her trade. She cleaned them off with a rag and put them away. Mitch grabbed her arm. She hadn't seen him approach again. He pulled her back over. She grabbed the vice grips on the way. Apparently, she had more work to do.

After a little more squeezing the flow of answers continued. She wished she could understand what they were talking about.

Some of the men punched their captive from time to time.

She put her last tool away and closed her bag.

Mitch motioned for her to follow him into the adjoining room.

Ariadne had no idea how long it had lasted, but it must have been a few hours.

"That should be it," Mitch told her. "You can go now. If we need you anymore, I'll call you."

He handed her an envelope.

She folded it, put it in her bag.

"Do you want to take a shower?"

She nodded. The men in the other room had stopped yelling. They were still talking, but their voices were lower now.

"Are you sure I'm done this time?" she asked. "I just want to take a shower and go home."

"For tonight," Mitch said. "Yeah."

"Good."

He opened the door, and she slipped out, heading to the bathroom.

Ariadne closed that door and locked it. As she washed herself, she closed her eyes, she tried to block out everything, the entire world, and let the hot water rain on her.

She didn't want to be here.

There was blood on her clothes despite her precautions, and she rinsed them in the sink after her shower. She'd brought a change of clothes, wrapped in plastic, in her tool bag. She got dressed and unlocked the door.

The men were still huddled around their prisoner.

She moved quietly past them. Mitch caught her eye and kind of half-waved. Ariadne pretended not to notice and slipped out the door. She went as quickly as she could past the checkpoints and didn't bother to call for a cab from the lobby. She walked until she was a block away, and hailed one then.

CHAPTER 21

Merry and Lilac were in bed, wrapped around each other and in the sheets, watching a video of one of her earlier films. There she was, two years younger, fucking a blonde girl whose name she couldn't remember with a strap-on dildo.

"You ever think about becoming a real actress?" Merry asked.

"Aw, come on," Lilac said. "I'm awful. I can't even pull *these* shitty lines off. I sound so fucking affected."

"I think you're cute," Merry said. "Damn cute. And you have a real *something*. You know, screen presence. And you're no worse than some of the morons who're making Hollywood movies these days."

"You think so?"

"Some of these young actors today, they have a pretty face and that's about it. They have no *substance* to them, no reality. They're just these attractive ghosts, floating up there on screen. Not like the old days. You catch any of the old movies, you see real stars. Real people, at least more real than the shit today. Bogart, William Holden, Dietrich, even Marilyn. They had this something *extra*. The stars today are just mannequins."

"You really like old movies, huh?"

"Sure," Merry said. "It's funny. Movies have gotten more realistic over the years. Language, sex. Don't get me wrong, there are still good movies being made, and good actors, but they're rare, especially since the end of the 70s. You have to look harder for them now. But the old movies, the old black and white ones, maybe they were more sanitized and all, but the people were more real. More believable. People used to say Marilyn

Monroe was a lousy actress, but she acted circles around most of the bitches making millions today."

"Do you think I have any of the stuff Marilyn had?"

"You're real," Merry said.

"That's because I'm here with you. You can feel me. Of course you know I'm real." She pinched him.

"Hey!"

"See what I mean? Don't go flattering me about my acting, because I know it's just bullshit. I don't fool myself about it."

"Most people in porn act as well as those mannequins in the big Hollywood films."

"Oh come on!"

"Maybe not all of them."

She squeezed him tight. "Watch the movie. I almost forgot about this one. I hardly ever watch my own movies. It makes me feel funny. But I wanted to watch this with you. See how it felt."

"How does it feel?"

"Strange. But it kind of turns me on."

"Me too."

Lilac and the blonde girl in the movie were really going at it. They watched the TV screen in wide-eyed silence.

"You really like girls, huh?"

"Yeah, sure," Lilac said. "It doesn't bother me or nothing. You think you'd want to do something like that sometime? I know most guys fantasize about stuff like that."

"You mean a threesome?"

"Yeah," Lilac said. "I wouldn't mind. Hell, I've already done it in movies, lots of times. It would be fun to do it for real, and I know lots of girls who would be willing."

"Let me think about it," Merry said. "I want to concentrate on just you for the time being."

She smiled.

The scene ended, the two girls writhing in orgasm. And the movie shifted to a guy and a girl going at it in a motel room. The guy was Jack.

"Shit," Lilac said. "I forgot that fuckhead was in this."

She tried to get up to shut it off.

Merry stopped her.

"You don't want to see that prick in action, do you?" she asked.

"You don't have any scenes with him in this movie, do you?"

"No. I wasn't even on the set during his scenes. I've only had scenes with him two or three times, and I hated it each time. He's too rough and has bad breath."

He did, however, have a very big dick.

Merry sat up and grabbed the remote. He watched for a couple more minutes and then shut it off.

"So you grew up with that caveman? What was he like when you were kids?"

"Like I said before, an asshole," Merry said. "Same as now."

"The first time I met him, I couldn't stand him. He's like this self-absorbed, smug fuck who thinks women should be honored to be around him or something. He definitely gives that vibe, you know? Was he like that in high school?"

"I guess so," Merry said. "He used to date cheerleader types. I doubt he went without it much."

"What about you?"

"I was this quiet guy who kept to himself. I never went out for sports or any of that shit. I didn't care about any of that. It bored the shit out of me. I just tried to pass the time, you know. I couldn't wait for the years to go by, so I could get away from all that shit."

"I was kind of shy in school, too," Lilac said. "It was a Catholic girls' school. I wasn't in any of the cliques or anything, and I hardly had any opportunity to meet boys. I didn't really seek them out, you know. I only had one date the whole time I was in high school. He seemed nice enough, but as soon as he got me alone, he was all hands. I wasn't expecting it and it kind of freaked me out. When I put up a fight he lost interest and stopped calling me."

"Those hormones!" Merry said.

"I know," Lilac said. "I kind of feel sorry for him now. He was so hungry-like, you know? I told him to go jerk off."

"I did my share of that."

"Oh, a guy like you shouldn't have to."

"Come on, who's bullshitting now?" Merry asked. "I was a

big, quiet kid. People probably thought I was a retard."

"You're so cute though. I'd think you were hot, even if you were retarded."

"Gee, thanks a lot," Merry said. "So if you were so virginal in high school, how did you end up in porn?"

"I went to college for a couple of years," she said, and smiled. "Really, I did. And I wanted to make up for lost time. I guess I kind of got carried away."

"What a change," Merry said.

"I got pregnant," she went on. "And I dropped out of school. I didn't have the baby, but the whole thing kind of shook me up. About this time, a friend of mine was doing movies now and then, and I kind of let her talk me into going along with her. I didn't want to go back to school, and I didn't want to go back home. I wanted to make it on my own. And there weren't a lot of good paying jobs I was qualified for. And the ones I could have gotten, I didn't want. Really, I didn't know *what* I wanted. So I gave this a shot. I didn't think I'd stick with it, but I guess I kind of got hooked. I've been doing it almost three years now."

"You still like it?"

"Sure," she said. "It pays well, and there are times I really do enjoy it. Honest. Except for when I have to do things with jerks like Jack. I'm starting to learn I can say no a little more now and turn down things I don't like, though."

"So did you have a real bad home life?"

"I don't think it was so bad," Lilac said. "Not like some of the horror stories I've heard. I mean, my parents got divorced when I was young, but I learned to live with that. My mother had a lot of boyfriends. You know, these guys who'd stick around for months, but who'd always move on. I think my mother had a problem with commitment after the split with Dad. None of them ever molested me or anything. Not like it wasn't obvious some of them were *interested*. But they weren't abusive-type guys. My mother wouldn't have put up with that. So, no, I don't have any horror stories to tell you. I just kind of stumbled into this line of work and decided to stick with it for a while."

"What about diseases and shit?" Merry asked. "Especially these days. Don't you worry about that?"

"We all get blood tests pretty regularly. I know that sounds lame, but I feel kind of safe. I work for Tony a lot and he uses a lot of the same people. We're kind of like an insulated little group, you know."

"What about jerks like Jack? Do you trust them?"

"I'd be lying if I said I never worry about it. But I've been lucky so far. And I've been trying to do more girl-girl stuff, now that I have some seniority, or whatever you call it. I think that's a lot safer."

Merry had been worrying about it himself. He'd only known her two days, but they'd been fucking like hormone-crazed teenagers. He'd used condoms a few times, but there were a few frenzied times, when he'd just said *fuck it*. He trusted her more than he should have, maybe.

"Since this movie's done, I'll be going for a blood test tomorrow. Do you want to come with me and hold my hand?"

"Okay, sure."

"Thanks," she said. "It'll be nice to have the company."

"You ever think about giving it up?"

"I always thought if I found the right guy, maybe I'd give it up. But I never found anybody before who made me even think about it." She looked into his eyes and smiled.

"We just met and all," Merry said. "So I don't have any right to make any demands or anything."

"I just can't take a regular job, Merry. It would just depress the hell out of me. If I ever quit this, I have to have something I can replace it with. Something I can live with."

"I guess I understand."

"Besides, I thought you said you'd think about Tony's suggestion. He told me he mentioned maybe you and me doing a scene in his next picture. You interested? It'd be good money, and we'd have some fun."

"Let me think about it."

"Tony's a real nice guy. He's great to work for."

"Yeah," Merry said, distracted. "Hey, you talked about your mother. What about your father?"

"After him and mom split up, I saw him maybe once a year. He moved to another state and married a woman I couldn't stand. She had this bratty bitch from another marriage. All we'd do was fight on the holidays when I went to visit. It was awful.

"What were your parents like?" Lilac asked.

"Huh?"

"I told you about my parents. What were yours like?"

"I didn't know my father at all," Merry said. "He took off when I was still a baby."

"Oh, that's awful."

"I got by. My mother worked all these hours and stuff. Sometimes relatives watched me. I learned to raise myself, mostly. It wasn't so bad. I did okay."

"Looks like we both did okay, considering."

"We both did all right."

She squeezed him. "You want to watch my scenes again?" she asked him, jerking her head toward the TV. "I don't feel so weird watching them with you."

"Why don't we make our own scenes?"

CHAPTER 22

By the time Ariadne got home, the sun was up. It was almost eight o'clock.

She stripped her clothes off and turned on the shower. She'd already had one a few hours before, but she didn't feel clean. She scrubbed herself for almost half an hour. When she was done, and her skin was red from scrubbing, she toweled off and went out to the living room.

The message light on the answering machine was blinking. There could have been a message from Mitch, but she didn't feel like talking to him just yet. She also had a beeper, but she rarely used it, and had gotten grief for that. She didn't go out very much, and was easy enough to reach on the phone most of the time. But there were times she just wanted to be left alone.

She hadn't gone straight home after hailing the cab. The driver took her to the beach. She paid him and then walked along the shore.

Few other people were around. Couples jogging. A middle-aged man flying a kite. A couple of homeless people stirring beneath one section of the boardwalk. No one came near her. No one talked to her. She took off her shoes and walked along the shoreline, letting the water tickle her feet.

She enjoyed the peacefulness.

After walking as far along the beach as she could, she put her shoes back on and decided to walk home. It took about an hour. She got lost in her thoughts and didn't notice.

Looking at the message light blinking, Ariadne was tempted to pop the tape out and throw it away. Instead, she found herself pushing the "Play" button.

"Ariadne, this is Francie. I'm sorry to be calling so late, but I wanted to talk to you. Are you there? Well, I guess you're sleeping or at work. Give me a call back sometime, okay?"

Francie must have called while she was out. A second message was from her as well.

"Ariadne, it's me again. I'm not having much luck reaching you. Call me back soon, huh?"

Ariadne stood, staring down at the machine as it cleared its messages and reset itself.

Neither message was from Mitch. She sighed in relief. She couldn't tell if Francie was trying to reach her for a reason, or if she just wanted to talk, but it would have to wait. Ariadne was dead tired, and she needed sleep.

All the shades were drawn, the lights off as Ariadne walked naked through the apartment until she reached her bedroom.

She threw herself down on the bed and closed her eyes.

CHAPTER 23

Francie contemplated calling Ariadne a third time. She was dressed and ready to head off to work, but she had an odd feeling that something was wrong.

By looking at the facts, there was no real reason to worry.

She and Ariadne often went days without calling one another. Ariadne's job meant she worked odd hours and slept when she could. Francie was used to that. But something had told her to call the night before, and since she hadn't yet received a call back, she was getting worried.

She put the phone down, realizing she couldn't keep track of all of Ariadne's comings and goings. Ariadne was an adult who knew what she was doing and could take care of herself.

Maybe it was what Ariadne did for a living, but sometimes she was compelled to check up on her. Make sure she was all right.

Sometimes she had these feelings that something was wrong. She knew it was silly to put too much stock in them. But she couldn't shake it this time.

She looked at the time. She was running late. She picked the phone up again. She called the office and told them she would be there soon.

She thought about swinging by Ariadne's place on the way to work, but decided against it. Ariadne hated it when she got too protective. It was bad enough that she left two messages. She forced herself to let it go as she looked for her car keys.

CHAPTER 24

Merry sat in the waiting room, flipping through out-of-date fashion magazines. Lilac was getting her blood tested. He read the same paragraph about eight times and then he put the magazine down and stared at the walls.

He was not alone. The waiting room was full of women.

Some were teenagers, and others were older than he was. He tried not to look at any of them, at least not so they would notice.

Lilac hadn't taken long, and he stood and waited while she talked to the woman at the front desk, making an appointment for her next visit.

She came over and grabbed his hand. "Let's go," she said.

She led him out into the hall. Their footsteps reverberated on the hard tile. They stopped in front of the elevators.

"Don't tell me you're still nervous," Lilac said. "I do this all the time, and there's nothing to worry about. It's just a formality so I can keep working."

"I've never been in a place like this before," Merry said, looking around.

"A doctor's office?"

"No," Merry said. "You know what I mean."

"No, I don't," Lilac told him. "I've tried to reassure you all I can. What else can I say?"

"Maybe I shouldn't have come along."

"Maybe not," Lilac said, looking down at her shoes. "I wouldn't have asked you if I knew it would stress you out so much."

"How long does it take now?"

"For the results?" Lilac said. "About two weeks. But I told you there's nothing to worry about. God, I didn't know this would bother you so much!"

He didn't want to talk about it. The elevator doors opened and he entered first, not even realizing he was still holding her hand until she almost stumbled beside him.

"Sorry," Merry said.

"Actually, I'm sorry," Lilac said. "For bringing you here."

Merry was going to say something reassuring, but he couldn't think of anything. They just stood there, and then he realized they hadn't pushed the button for their floor. Lilac leaned forward and pressed it.

"I got paid yesterday," Lilac said. "How about we go out for lunch, my treat? What kind of food do you like?"

"My stomach's bothering me," Merry said. "I don't think I'm up for lunch just yet."

She looked up into his eyes. Her eyes were filmy, on the verge of tears. "I'm really fucking this up, aren't I?" she asked. "I finally meet a great guy and I'm making a mess of it."

"No, not at all," Merry said.

"Do you still want me to stick around?" she asked him.

"Of course I do," he said, as the elevator doors opened.

They walked out into the lobby, still holding hands.

"I'm not much for eating right now," Merry said. "But I could go for a drink. How about you?"

"Okay," Lilac said. "Let's go get plastered!"

CHAPTER 25

Jack Underwood nuzzled his lover's breast with his face. He playfully pulled at her skin with his lips and then bared his teeth for a bite.

The woman did not react as he bit her, but there was a good reason for that. She was dead.

They were in the bathroom, in his extra big tub. He had cut her in several places and bled her out. Her blood was all over him.

He would have a lot of cleaning to do, but it didn't bother him. Cleaning relaxed him. Jack had another hard-on. He grabbed the container of lube on the counter beside him. When he entered her, she was still slightly warm. He even kissed her, getting caught up in the fantasy.

After he came, he collapsed on top of her and wrapped his arms around her. Her warmth was fading, and he wanted what was left all for himself.

When she started to get cold and stiff, he pulled himself off and stood up. He turned on the shower and washed himself, as she lay beneath him. Then he carefully walked out into the hall and began getting things out of the closet: a bucket, mop, and a bottle of ammonia. He filled the bucket in the sink with hot water.

Then from the linen closet he grabbed a couple of clean sheets to wrap the body in.

He went back into the bathroom and lifted her body out of the tub and placed it down on the floor, on the sheets. He wrapped her carefully and rolled her into the corner of the room.

He added ammonia to the bucket and started cleaning. *This place is going to be spotless*, Jack thought.

CHAPTER 26

Someone was pounding on the door.

Ariadne had no idea how long it had been going on. She had been in a deep sleep and didn't realize the sounds were real until they pulled her into the waking world.

She lay there with her eyes open, not wanting to move.

The pounding continued.

Ariadne pulled herself out of bed and moved slowly toward the door. Her head was foggy and she didn't think to put on any clothes.

She stopped in front of the door. The chain lock wasn't on, but the dead bolt was, and she didn't see anything through the peephole. "Is anyone there?" she asked, but got no reply.

She put the chain on, turned the lock, and pulled the door open a few inches, looking out into the hall.

A man standing near the door shoved his hands toward her.

She should have been more cautious, should have gotten her gun before she answered the door. But the man was not trying to attack her. He collapsed against the wall, and she took the chain off. She went out into the hallway. It crossed her mind as she brought him inside her apartment that this might be some kind of trick, but by then it was too late. Dammit, she wasn't thinking clearly.

His hands were covered with burns and cuts, and in the center of each hand was a horrendous wound, like some terrible stigmata. The wounds had started healing over, but were puckered and still pretty disturbing to look at.

Ariadne stared at the hands, unable to move. And then her eyes darted to the face, and she recognized him.

It was a man she had interrogated a week ago.

His name was Fredericks. She had nailed his hands to a wall.

There were cigarette burns on his face. Scars. His face was in as horrible shape as his hands. And it was all because of *her*. She had done these things to him.

He stirred and started struggling, but, he was very weak. She left him on the floor and looked out in the hallway again, to make sure nobody was watching. She didn't see anyone. She went back into the apartment and turned the lock. She slid the chain in place. *How the fuck did he get here?* she wondered. *How did he escape from captivity? How does he know where I live?*

She went to her bedroom and put on a robe, and she got her gun. Then she grabbed the phone and called Mitch's number.

The phone rang. Once, twice.

"Hello," the voice on the other side said. "Hello?"

"Merry?" she asked. In her panic, she had dialed the wrong number.

"Ariadne?" Merry asked. "Is that really you?"

He sounded like he'd been drinking, like he wasn't sure he could believe what he was hearing.

"Sorry," she said, and hung up. She dialed again.

This time she was certain she'd dialed the right number.

It rang.

She took a deep breath.

It rang several more times. No answer.

Ariadne went back into the other room. The front door was open and Fredericks was gone. She could hear some kind of struggle in the hallway. She went out in the hall and watched as some men carried him down the stairs.

She stood there a long time, watching where they had gone. She was about to go back inside her apartment, when someone else came up the stairs. It was Mitch. He did not look happy.

"Pack a bag and come with me," he said.

PART II

CHAPTER 27

It was one in the afternoon, and Merry was sucking on a beer bottle, thinking about Ariadne. That night two weeks ago, when she'd called him. She was the last person he ever expected to hear from again. And she'd sounded so upset, so scared. He'd never heard her like that before. She had always been so sure of herself, *so in control.*

He'd told Lilac he had to go, and he'd gotten in his car and driven to her place. It felt strange going back to that part of town, and yet, in another way, it was like going home. She'd kept the apartment they had lived in together. It was a better neighborhood, and he missed it sometimes.

He stood downstairs, ringing her buzzer, getting no answer. He tried the main door. It was unlocked. So he went inside the building.

He climbed the stairs. The building was so quiet. There was no one in the hallway, and he knocked on her door.

He knocked a few more times and then got out his key chain.

He still had a key from when he'd lived here, even though he hadn't used it since they separated. He was surprised when it still worked; he had thought she would have changed the locks.

He went inside.

The apartment was a lot like he remembered it. She hadn't changed it much. But then again, most of it had been her choice. He hadn't cared enough to disagree with any of it.

Back then, all he'd cared about was being with her.

He checked all the rooms, but she wasn't here. The place was in disarray, like she'd been in a hurry to leave. There weren't any signs of a struggle, but it bothered him because she had always been so orderly. Everything in its place, and all that shit. It had driven him nuts sometimes, but he'd put up with anything for her.

Back then.

That was before he found out what she did for a living. She'd told him she worked for the city, and he'd let it go at that. Until that day he had found her special bag, quite by accident. He'd gone through it, and even then he wasn't sure just what it all meant.

So he confronted her, and she told him everything. It wasn't like she was some kind of criminal. But her work wasn't something she was encouraged to discuss with anyone, either. She told him it had been difficult keeping secrets from him for so long.

He asked her what she used some of the tools for, and she told him that, too.

He never felt the same about her after that. It created a chasm between them that grew until it got too big, and then things were over between them.

She'd been so warm once. He hadn't suspected she had that other side to her. He couldn't believe she was capable of such cruelty. And she didn't seem to have any problem with it.

Maybe that was what bothered him most.

He was in her apartment, where they used to live together, and she was gone. And the way she had sounded on the phone, that moment of vulnerability, reminded him of what she had been like when they had first met. The girl he'd fallen in love with.

He'd almost convinced himself *that* version of Ariadne still existed.

On his way out, he noticed there were little flecks of what looked like blood on the living room carpet. Not much, but it scared him. He thought about calling the police. He even knew who he'd ask for—Manny, his old partner. But even before he picked up the phone, he abandoned the idea.

Two things stopped him. The first was that she worked for the government. Well, he *thought* it was the government. He couldn't be completely sure *who* they were. That was one of the few things she wouldn't tell him. And when he had tried to investigate it on his own, he hadn't gotten very far. Whoever it was, they didn't want to be scrutinized. Either way, he didn't want to get Manny, or anyone else, in over his head. Better to just leave it alone.

The second was that he was kind of afraid of Ariadne. He knew if he stuck his nose where it didn't belong, she'd be angry. And she was alien to him now. He had no idea what her reaction would be. She was so hung up on taking care of herself. Of not needing anyone.

So even though she'd sounded scared on the phone, he talked himself out of getting involved. She didn't look to him for protection. He wasn't responsible for her welfare anymore.

But why had she called him?

Confused, he left the apartment as he had found it and locked up. He quietly walked downstairs and locked the outside door on his way out.

Back home, he had called Ariadne's place a few times. The first time, there was no answer. Not even an answering machine. The second time, a woman speaking Spanish answered. It wasn't her. She had changed her number.

He just wanted to hear her voice, make sure everything was okay, but eventually, he tried to forget about it, *tried* being the operative word.

Merry stood there, thinking about it all, when Lilac let herself in.

"Drinking already?"

"Hi," he said. "Where have you been?"

"Nice greeting," Lilac said. "And after I made sure I didn't wake you this morning. You looked so peaceful sleeping. I had things to do."

"Like what?"

"I went to the clinic and got my results," she said. "I'm clean. No diseases."

"I almost forgot about that."

"No you didn't."

"All right, I didn't. That's good news."

"And I did a little shopping." She dropped the bags she was

carrying and reached inside one, took out a smaller bag, and handed it to him. "Here."

"What's that?"

"Just take it," Lilac said. "I'm sorry I didn't have a chance to wrap it."

He opened the bag and pulled out a little box. Inside was a silver chain. "What's this for?"

"That key of yours," Lilac said. "You keep it on that shoelace. I wanted to get you something nicer."

"It's nicer all right."

"I was going to get you gold, but I pegged you for a silver guy. I figured you'd think gold was too gaudy."

"You pegged me right."

"Put it on."

He took the string necklace off and put the silver chain through the hole in the head of the key. He put it back around his neck again.

"It looks nice," she told him.

"Yeah," he said. "Thanks."

"I was going to get a necklace with something else on it. Something more exciting than a key, but I thought you wouldn't like that."

"Probably not."

"What's the appeal of that key, anyway?"

"I already told you all that."

"I guess so," Lilac said.

"Trying to change me already, huh?" Merry asked.

"I know when I'm beat," she said. "I got you some new clothes, too. I checked your sizes while you were sleeping."

"You want something to drink?"

"I was thinking we could go somewhere special, celebrate my news."

"What news?"

"My test results," Lilac said. "Where have *you* been?"

"Maybe you should save your money. You don't want to spend it all on me."

"Why not?" Lilac said. "I'm fine, money-wise. The rent's all paid up. We've got plenty of food. What's the problem?"

Merry finished his beer and went to get another one.

"Any luck finding a job?"

"No," Merry said from the other room. "Not yet."

"Have you been looking?"

"Sure I have."

"Really?"

"Sometimes," Merry said, coming back in with a fresh beer. "Hell, I don't have any idea what I want to do anymore."

"I talked to Tony today."

Merry took a long pull on the bottle.

"Have you thought over what he asked you?"

"Not really," Merry said.

"Why not?"

"I don't know how I feel about it."

"It'll be you and me," Lilac said.

"And a camera," he said. "I know."

"Nothing to be afraid of. And it's good money."

"So you talked to him," Merry said. "That mean you're going back to work soon?"

"I was going to talk to you first."

"Why?" Merry asked. "It's not up to me."

"It is if you want to do a scene with me. Besides, we're together now."

"Let me sleep on it."

"Okay," Lilac said. "But I need an answer soon. Tony wants me to call him before the end of the week."

"Where's the filming going to be?" Merry asked. "Next door again?"

"I don't know," Lilac said. "Probably not. I think they want to use a new location. Does it matter?"

"No, I guess not."

"Come on," Lilac said. "Let's go get something to eat."

"Yeah, you wanted to celebrate. Do you celebrate every time you pass a blood test?"

"Actually, I do. I'm superstitious that way, I guess. Besides, it's a big relief."

"Well, there is an easier way."

Lilac didn't say anything to that.

"Let's go later," Merry said. "I'm not up for it right now."

"What's wrong?"

"I don't know," he said.

"Try on some of the clothes I got you."

"I'm in a weird mood, I guess."

"You're probably just buzzed."

"Maybe."

Lilac picked up her bags and disappeared inside the bedroom. Merry turned on the radio and listened to music while he finished another beer.

CHAPTER 28

"Here's your drink."

Ariadne shifted on the blanket and rolled onto her side. She looked up at Mitch and took the glass. "Thanks."

"Sure thing," he said. "You getting enough sun?"

"Too much, probably."

"You know, you really look great."

"So you keep telling me," she said, looking over his lean, muscular, and tanned physique. "You're no slouch yourself."

He smiled. She was getting really used to that smile.

Ariadne sat up and put the glass to her mouth. She drank it down a little faster than she should have.

"My, my," Mitch said. "You really were thirsty."

"Parched."

Ariadne was wearing a string bikini, and gritty sand rubbed against her skin as she moved. It had been so long since she'd spent any time on a beach. Years. And here they'd spent the better part of two weeks on one. She was lucky she didn't get any bad burns. Mitch took care of that. It was his job to rub suntan oil on her.

To think something bad happening had led to this little getaway. Fredericks and two other captives had somehow escaped; it looked like Mitch's ass would be in a sling. But he and his partners had rounded them up and managed to put a lid on the whole thing. After that, Mitch suggested they get away, just the two of them, to put some distance between them and what had happened. Ariadne had been shaken up and agreed maybe a little too quickly.

Now she was glad she did.

She didn't realize how badly she needed a vacation until they got to the Bahamas. She had been here once before, as a child, with her parents. But it was nothing like this time. This time, it was almost like a honeymoon. Just her and Mitch. No more arguments, no more mating dances. The little crisis back home had been enough to open her up, to make her just vulnerable enough to let her guard down.

And Mitch was clearly taking full advantage of that. Not that she minded.

"Can I have another drink?" she asked.

"So soon?"

"Why not? Do we have to be somewhere or something?" She laughed and handed the glass to him.

"I guess we can't go swimming now, huh?" Mitch asked her.

"You go along."

"You know I hate to swim alone," he said.

"Tough."

"What do you have against the water?"

"I guess I'm just like a cat," she told him. "And you're like a fish."

"Makes sense," he said. "You're a Leo and I'm a Pisces, after all."

"You're so silly. I never did believe any of that horoscope crap," she said.

"I got you to go swimming when we first got here."

"I was giddy with excitement then," Ariadne said. "You could have talked me into anything."

"What I mean is, you know how to swim."

"So?"

"Come on!"

"Unless you want us to have our first lover's spat, I'd suggest you just drop it."

"Lover's spat," he said. "I like the sound of that."

There was suddenly a glimmer of mischief in his eyes. "Do I have to pick you up and carry you in?"

"You try, and I'll break a rib."

"You're not serious."

"Try me."

He laughed and tried to scoop her up in his arms. She struggled and then hit him in the arm to make him stop. It was just hard enough.

"You're serious."

"No shit."

"You know, sometimes you can be a real stick in the mud."

"Tough shit."

"Maybe I'll go get that drink, now," he said.

"Sounds good to me."

"I never met anyone like you before," Mitch said. "And I'm not sure if that's good or bad."

"Tell me again the next time we're fucking," she told him.

He laughed. When he laughed like that, he was just so fucking cute she had to smile.

"You need some more suntan lotion?" Mitch asked.

"Maybe when you get back."

He had been crouching beside her, and now he stood up. "It's so beautiful here."

"Yeah," Ariadne said. "It's heavenly. I'm so glad you suggested it."

"It was a great idea of mine, wasn't it?"

"I was just thinking how it's been years since I had a real vacation."

"Didn't you ever go on trips when you were married?"

She had told him about Merry. They'd talked about a lot of things since they got here. Things she had never mentioned before because she'd wanted to keep her personal life private. In a way it felt good to open up to someone. Someone besides Francie, that is.

"No," she said. "We wouldn't think to come to a place like this. And Merry, he hated to travel. Absolutely hated it. We went to Mexico for our honeymoon. And we went to Europe once, early on in our marriage. For a couple of weeks. All he did was bitch and moan about how nothing was as good as it was back home. I'm surprised I was able to talk him into those two trips. After that, I just stopped suggesting we do any traveling, and he seemed relieved by that."

"Doesn't sound like much fun."

"Merry and I, we were a lot alike," Ariadne said. "Solitary kind of people, you know. We really did get along pretty well most of the time."

"Until he found out what you did for a living."

"Yeah," she said. "It really freaked him out."

"Did you ever offer to give it up?"

"No."

"Why not?"

"Because what I do is part of me. For better or worse. If he couldn't deal with it, we were better off apart."

"You can be a real tough customer when you want to be."

"I'm glad you know that," Ariadne said. "Lets you know what you're up against."

"I think I can handle it."

"Do you?"

"I'm going to enjoy finding out."

They both laughed.

"How about that drink?" she asked.

"Coming right up, ma'am."

He walked back to the bar. Ariadne stretched out on her back again and closed her eyes.

For some odd reason, she thought about that phone call she had made by accident, the night when everything was chaos. When she'd called Merry. It had been so long since she'd seen him, heard from him. She wondered what his reaction had been, hearing her voice again. Maybe she should call him when they got home, let him know everything was okay. She didn't know how she sounded on the phone, if he would be worried or not. She hoped not.

The sun was hot on her brow. She thought of Mitch fucking her in their hotel room. It had been a while since she'd had any kind of normal relationship, and she had really needed it. She'd almost forgotten how much she missed regular sex.

Almost.

Merry had been pretty good in bed too, until they both started to get lazy. And toward the end, when he'd been acting so strange, their sex life had been almost nonexistent.

How could the way he had felt about her change so

drastically? He was like some kind of alien creature at the end. When he left, he took the tension with him. And for that reason, she had been glad to see him go.

But they had shared something special once. And she missed that.

"You're not sleeping, are you?" Mitch asked.

His shadow blocked the sun. She opened her eyes and stared up at him.

Mitch was younger than Merry, and in better shape. And he was so energetic in bed. Fucking him was like an Olympic sport.

"I'm sorry about not wanting to go swimming," she said.

"That's okay," he said. "I can go alone."

"I can think of something else we can do together," she said, smiling. "Something even better than swimming."

"Oh, can you?"

She sat up, and he handed her the glass.

"Let's pack this stuff up and head back to our room."

"Just like that?"

"Just like that," she said. She drained the glass again. He seemed surprised at this. Merry wouldn't have even blinked. The two of them had had drinking marathons on occasion, and she'd been able to match Merry drink for drink.

Mitch's facial expression made her laugh.

"What's so funny?" Mitch asked.

"Oh, I don't know," Ariadne said, thinking about it and not wanting to come off like a lush. She barely had a buzz, but she said, "I guess the alcohol is just going to my head."

He grabbed her hand and tried to help her up.

"Why don't we just do it right here?" she asked him.

He looked around at the other people on the beach and back at the bar. "In front of all these people?" he asked. "That must be the alcohol talking."

"Maybe," she said. She got to her feet, and wiped sand off her skin. "How much longer can we stay here?"

"Another day or two," Mitch said. "Then we have to get back. So let's make the most of it."

"Let's," she agreed.

CHAPTER 29

"I met my father once," Merry said.

They were wrapped in a sheet, leaning back on pillows. He had his arm around Lilac.

"You did?" she asked. "I thought you said you never knew your father."

"I never knew him, but I met him. Just once."

"When?"

"I must have been about fourteen, maybe."

"How did you meet him?" Lilac asked, a little annoyed at the way she had to tug the story out of him.

"Me and a pal of mine, we beat him up in a parking lot."

She stared at him. "How did you know it was him?"

"I'd seen a picture. My mother had this picture of him. It was one of the few things she had of his. I found it once. So I knew it was him. A little older, but it was him."

"Did he know who you were?"

"No," Merry said. "I don't think so."

"Why did you do it?"

"I hated him. He'd left my mother when I was born. He'd abandoned us. He never tried to get in touch with me. Never even called me on Christmas."

"So you beat him up."

"Yeah. We punched him, kicked him. He was in pretty bad shape when we took off. I don't think he'd had a chance to get a good look at us. But I got a good look at him. He was putting some grocery bags in his car. That part of the parking lot was pretty deserted, so I took advantage of it. I paid him back good."

"Did he live near you and your mother?"

"I was visiting my friend Phil; he lived a few towns over. I never did find out where my father lived. I never saw him again. Phil never saw him again either, and he told me he looked."

"How did you feel after you did it?"

"I don't know. I guess I was kind of numb after it happened."

"That's some story."

"I never told anyone that before," Merry said. "Not even my ex-wife."

Lilac looked over at him. "What made you tell me?"

"I don't know. I feel really calm around you. And I guess I wanted to finally get it off my chest. Maybe I just wasn't ready to tell anyone until now."

"Did your mother ever tell you anything about your father? Do you know anything about him?"

"No," Merry said. "She never mentioned him. I found that picture by accident. She was kind of upset when I asked her who it was. It was my grandmother who told me. She must have been visiting or something. I didn't care for her much. She could be one mean lady. But she told me who the guy in the picture was."

"Did she tell you anything else?"

"She said my father was gay. That he left my mother to chase other men."

"Oh, man!" Lilac said.

"I don't know if I believed her or not," Merry said. "Like I said, she was a mean old bitch. She might have just said that to be mean, you know? I guess I didn't care. I wanted to believe it because I hated him, and when you're young and stupid you can convince yourself to hate people who are gay because you're so unsure of who you are. Of who you're going to be. So it just gave me another reason to hate him. I feel pretty lousy about it now."

"So when you did see him, you had all this anger."

"Yeah," Merry said. "He didn't put up much of a fight. He didn't say a word. It was almost like he knew he had it coming."

"So what do you feel about it now?"

"Now?" Merry said. "I regret it more than anything else I ever did in my life. It was the only time I ever saw him. I could have talked to him. I could have asked him why he took off. I could have gotten his side of things. Maybe I could have understood things better then. I could have given him a chance to be my father."

Lilac lit a cigarette. She passed it to Merry. He took a drag, and she lit up another one for herself.

"I'll probably never get that chance again," Merry said.

"I knew my father," Lilac said. "I guess he could be okay. But I never felt close to him. I don't know if I ever loved him. He was just someone I had to visit once or twice a year. Someone I really didn't want to see."

"We're a lot alike, you and me," Merry said.

"Yeah."

Merry hugged her closer.

"Thanks for telling me," Lilac said. "For trusting me."

"Sure."

"Don't let it bother you too much," she said. "You were just a kid. You didn't know how to handle things."

"I know," Merry said. "But when I think back on it, I still feel like shit."

"You don't know," Lilac said. "Maybe he was a total asshole. Maybe he *did* deserve it."

"I hope so," Merry said. "Either way, it's the one thing in my life I'm most ashamed of."

CHAPTER 30

When Francie got home from the office, she found a post-card in the mail from Ariadne. On the front was a beautiful picture of a beach at sunrise. On the back, she'd written, "All is well, having a great time. See you soon, Ariadne."

Francie stared at the handwriting, wondering if maybe it was someone playing a joke on her.

Ariadne had never mentioned a desire to go to the Bahamas. And she didn't seem like the kind of person who would enjoy sitting on a beach, getting sun. It just didn't sound like her at all.

But it was Ariadne's handwriting all right.

Francie went inside and put the postcard down on her coffee table.

Another postcard had arrived almost two weeks ago, right after Ariadne had disappeared. It had a picture of an airplane on the front. On the back she'd written, "Please don't worry. Everything is fine. I just needed to get away from it all. Talk to you soon."

Francie sat on the sofa and turned both postcards over to examine the photos.

It had been so sudden, Ariadne taking off like that. But that was the way she was. Impulsive. In a way, Francie was hurt because Ariadne hadn't asked her to go along. And she hadn't bothered to call.

Could it be she had gone with someone else? Maybe that guy Mitch she had been talking about?

Francie went into the kitchen and poured herself a glass of wine.

Her day at work had gone awful. She'd been on the phone

with a disgruntled client most of the day, and she had a whopper of a headache.

After work, some of the girls from the office were going out for drinks, but Francie went home. Her head was pounding, and she wanted to get as far away from the office as she could.

Besides, she missed Ariadne.

She knew it was foolish. She knew Ariadne did not feel the same way about her. But she wanted to be with her so badly.

Francie took the wine bottle and the glass and sat on the sofa. She looked down at the two postcards.

"Get a grip, Francie," she told herself. "She's probably having the time of her life with that Mitch guy."

She turned on the television. She switched channels until she saw a commercial for some travel agency. There was a couple on the beach, kissing.

Francie closed her eyes and thought of being on that beach with Ariadne, kissing her.

She took off her clothes and lay them out on the floor.

Then she got back on the couch and closed her eyes and thought about that beach again as she brought herself to orgasm.

CHAPTER 31

Mitch sat at the little writing desk in the room. He'd turned the chair to face the bed and was watching Ariadne sleep. She looked so peaceful, so innocent. A sleeping princess who'd gotten a nice bronze tan over the last two weeks.

And he thought about what she did for a living. He'd seen her do some pretty brutal things. She'd done it easily, without hesitation. And if those things didn't work, she did *worse* things. He had to admit she had talent. She was good at dishing out pain. And here she was, oblivious to the world and as far removed from that pain merchant he'd seen in action as she could get. She was a warm, sensual woman. He'd seen a side of her that was remarkable. In her work she was proficient, almost inhuman. Here she was totally human. From the noises she made during sex to playful kisses on his neck, she was absolutely human.

It amazed him how two such diametrically opposed sides could coexist in the same person. Yet she was perfectly sane.

He watched her sleep and thought she was someone he could fall in love with.

He thought back to when he was a kid, the kinds of girls he went after. They were pretty. Some might have been acting dumber than they were, to get the guys, but on the whole, they were pretty vacuous. And he was happy to get *that*. But Ariadne was like another fucking planet. She was smart, probably smarter than he was. She was complex. She could be totally ruthless. When he was a kid, he couldn't even dream of a girl like her. He didn't even know they existed.

But here she was, and he had made love to her countless

times, and she had been so warm and tender. So hungry and passionate.

It was like he'd done something incredible, getting her to come with him to this place. Like he'd tamed a wild animal.

A tigress.

But she was never really tame. She could revert to her wild ways at any moment.

She stirred, and he shifted in his seat.

She opened her eyes but didn't move. She didn't even swivel her head to see him better. She just stared into space, like a mesmerized cobra.

"You awake?" he asked softly.

She turned to face him. He sat back and opened his legs wider. To show her his hard-on.

She smiled.

"This is our last day here," he said. "What do you want to do?"

She stared at his cock and continued to smile.

"Well?"

She didn't move.

"I guess I'll get dressed then?"

"Don't you dare!" she said.

"Why don't you go back to sleep?"

"Come here."

He hesitated.

"Get your ass over here!"

He didn't move.

"Damn you," she said.

Ariadne kicked off the sheets and sat up. She faced him. He was sitting there with his erection pointing straight up.

Without another word, she ran over and mounted him.

He didn't resist. *Why would he?*

She was sliding up and down on him. He just sat there, watching her. Watching the intense look on her face as she fucked him.

Her teeth were clenched, like she was angry. Like she was trying to fuck him to death.

When they were done, she leaned forward and put her

arms around him, hugging him in the chair.

They closed their eyes and enjoyed the moment.

"That was a great way to start the day," Mitch said.

Ariadne just sighed.

CHAPTER 32

"I've been thinking about what you asked me," Merry said. "About doing that movie with you."

"Yeah?"

"Yeah," he said. "I think I want to do it."

"If you don't feel comfortable with the idea, you don't have to do it."

"I think I want to," Merry said. "I could use the money, you know. And it sounds like fun. I mean, once I get used to the idea of other people being around, watching us."

"It'll be strange at first, but I'll help you through it."

"If I do this, that'll be your only scene with a guy, right? Just me?"

"Sure," Lilac said. "You'll be the only guy."

"Can you promise me that?"

"Sure," Lilac said. "I promise."

"Then tell Tony I'll do it."

"Great."

"How long before shooting?"

"About two weeks."

"What do you want to do until then?"

"I don't know. I don't really have any plans." But if you want to do this, you'll have to get a blood test, anyway," she said.

"I know," he said, not sounding too thrilled about that. "But that won't take long. I have this friend. Phil. I told you about him, remember? I haven't seen him in a long time. A couple of years. But we stay in touch. Call each other on the phone sometimes. I've been wanting to go visit him for a while."

"You want to go now?"

"Do you want to go?"

"Sure," Lilac said. "Like I told you, I'm free. Anything you want to do."

"Where are we shooting? Around here?"

"I don't know yet," she said. "I'm waiting to hear from Tony."

"I guess it doesn't matter," Merry said. "It's about twelve hours to drive there. You want to tart packing?"

"I don't have much to pack. I brought my bags over here. That's all I've got."

"When's the last time you had your own place?" Merry asked.

"Long time ago," she said. "I've been living out of suitcases for more than a year now. Move to a new site, stay with friends until the shoot. Or people I work with. Then afterward move to the next location. All my travel's paid for."

"Well, after we do that movie, I want to look for a new apartment. Something nice. A place for the two of us."

"But you don't have a job yet."

"I'll get something," he said.

"Can I ask you something?" Lilac said. "Why did you leave the police force?"

"I shot a guy," he said. "An innocent bystander. It was an accident, and I was completely cleared for it. It wasn't negligence or anything. But I'd never shot anyone before, especially not an innocent person, and it fucked with my head. I tried to just go on with the job, I even went to therapy for a while; it was mandatory anyway. But the more I thought about it, the more I realized that it wasn't what I wanted to do with my life."

"So how are you paying the bills now? Some kind of pension?"

"I was only on the force eight years," Merry said. "But when my mother died, she left me some money. It was right about the time I was having second thoughts about being a cop. And her death just made me feel even worse. And I'd broken up with Ariadne, which complicated things further. So I decided to take some time off. And I've been feeling sorry for myself ever since. Until I met you."

The phone rang.

"Who'd call first thing in the morning?"

"Maybe it's Tony," Lilac said. "But I doubt it. He doesn't get up this early."

Merry thought maybe it was Ariadne. He didn't know why. Maybe he just wanted to hear from her, make sure she was okay.

He slid out of bed. It rang for the third time, and he picked it up.

"Pull up your shade!"

"What?"

"Your shade," the man's voice said. "Pull it up. I want to see you and your girlfriend fucking."

It was the man across the way. Again.

"You sick fuck!" Merry said.

"I want to see you fucking your new girlfriend," the man said. "I've got a new camera and I want to get some shots of your dick."

"You fucking asshole," Merry said. "I'll come over there and break your fucking neck!"

"Don't you dare come over here again," the man said. "I've got a gun. And I'm not afraid to use it."

"You won't get a chance to use it," Merry said.

"Just pull up the fucking shade!" the man said, and laughed really loud. Then he hung up.

"Who was it?" Lilac said.

He looked at the window. The shade was up a little bit. He hurried over and pulled it all the way down.

She was naked, standing in the doorway. "What's the big deal?" Lilac asked. "We're on the third floor."

"So is he," Merry said.

"Who?"

"Some fucking pervert across the way," Merry said. "His name is Finch. He spies on me. Calls me on the phone."

"How did he get your number?"

"He found out my name and looked it up, I guess. It's in the phone book." Merry said. "He's a psycho. I'm going to go over there and kill him one of these days."

"I'll take a shower," Lilac said. "Then we can ake a quick trip to the clinic." She didn't sound upset to find out she was being watched.

"That sounds okay."

"Want to take a shower with me? It will take your mind off that moron."

"Sure," Merry said, looking her over. "You go and start without me. I'll be right in."

"Okay," Lilac said. "But don't be long. Just put that asshole out of your mind."

"Okay," Merry said.

She walked to the bathroom. He unplugged the phone.

He returned to the bedroom and went to the window. He pushed the shade aside a little and peeked out.

The guy was over there, looking out his window with binoculars. Plain as day.

Merry could have reported the guy. He thought about calling some old friends of his on the force, have them throw a scare into him. Maybe when they got back from their trip.

"I'd better get out of here soon," Merry told himself. "Before I end up killing that guy."

CHAPTER 33

Jack Underwood parked in front of the abandoned house. He looked around. No one walking around. He headed for the trunk and retrieved a package. A big one. Then he went inside.

The stairs creaked almost as much as the doors. It was dark inside, but he knew his way around. He'd come to this house a lot when he was a kid. It was deserted even then. All the kids in the neighborhood played here, until Tommy Jackson fell through a rotted floorboard and almost died.

As kids they shared stories about this place. Said it was haunted.

They were probably right.

The walls were cracked, like the floors. No one had kept this place up, and no one had ever bought it. It was a mausoleum, standing in the same spot forever, waiting for the dead.

The dead Jack brought.

No kids played here now. There weren't that many kids in the neighborhood anymore. Most of the families had moved away years ago. It was so dilapidated even bums were afraid to stay here.

Animals weren't as skittish. More than once he'd found a stray dog in here, its snout covered in gore, feeding on a carcass it had ripped through plastic to find. Or rats. Rats weren't scared of anything except going hungry.

There were other abandoned buildings in the neighborhood now.

He stood in the doorway that led down to the cellar.

He didn't bother with the lights because they hadn't worked in a long time. The early morning light that crept in from outside gave him just enough illumination to get the job done.

He put the package over his shoulder. It was a good thing he worked out all the time to stay in shape. There were metal barrels down there. One of the empty ones was just waiting to be filled.

It was a cold morning. He could see his own breath.

When he was done filling the barrel, he went back upstairs.

He looked around as early morning daylight came in through the cracked windows. He'd played in this house as a child. It had never hurt him—not like it had Tommy Jackson. He felt safe here. It felt familiar. It was a good place to keep his secrets.

He went outside and got into his car. Looking around, he saw no one up and about yet. This neighborhood had gone to pot, and the people who had stuck around tended to sleep late. As late as they could. They were in no hurry to start another day.

But *he* couldn't wait for a new day. He ate them up like candy.

CHAPTER 34

"You all packed?" Mitch asked.

"I'm packed," Ariadne said. "Unfortunately."

"I know. It went by so fast."

"Too fast."

"Thanks for coming with me," Mitch said. "Really. When I asked you, I didn't know what your reaction would be. But I knew if you just gave me a chance, you'd see how good we are for each other."

She nodded. "Thanks for talking me into it. I really needed a break from everything. I needed to get away. And I'm glad I spent it with you. Seriously."

"I knew it," Mitch said.

"Don't congratulate yourself too much. I think I had something to do with this trip being such a success too."

"You sure did. And how!"

"So what happens now?"

"You tell me." He looked into her almost-purple eyes and tried to fall into them.

"Does this end here, or does it go on?" Ariadne asked. "Do we continue this back home?"

"That's up to you."

"Why up to *me*?"

"Because I'm in love with you, and I'll do whatever you want."

Ariadne seemed taken aback. "You mean that?"

"I don't say things like that very often," Mitch said. "Hell, I don't even know if I've ever said it before and actually meant it."

"Have you ever been married?"

"No. When I was younger, I never had any desire to. I got what I wanted without taking the plunge. And now, with the line of work we're in, I haven't had much time and opportunity to find anyone to get serious about."

"I know," Ariadne said. "It's tough."

"So where do I stand?"

"Let me think about it," Ariadne said, and smiled.

"You fucking tease!"

"What do you think about moving in together at some point?" she asked. "Do you think it's a good idea in our line of work?"

"I'm willing to test it out."

"Then let's test it," she said. "Let's see if this idyllic little getaway was just a fluke, or if we have what it takes to go the long haul."

"Sounds like fun."

"Fine," Ariadne said. "We'll sort things out when we get back."

Mitch moved closer and put his arms around her. He kissed her. "Thanks for giving me a chance, Ariadne."

"Just don't blow it."

"I won't."

"I'd like to take this a little further, but we have a plane to catch. We'd better get going."

"There are a lot of things we can do on a plane," Mitch told her, and kissed her again.

CHAPTER 35

It seemed as if they'd been driving forever.

The radio was on, some jazz station playing a long, experimental jam that didn't seem to want to end, and Lilac was asleep on the seat beside him.

It was starting to get dark, but they were making great time and were almost there. He'd called Phil earlier that morning to tell him he was coming and was bringing a friend. Phil had sounded genuinely happy. It had been a long time since they'd seen each other. There were a lot of things to catch up on.

The last time they'd seen each other was at Phil's wedding. Merry had still been with Ariadne, but things were icy with her, and they hadn't talked the whole way there and back.

Merry had no intension of going into detail about why he and Ariadne had split up. It just wasn't something he wanted to talk about. With Lilac along, it would be easier to avoid the subject.

Lilac stirred and adjusted her head where it rested on his shoulder.

The song on the radio had been going for at least twenty minutes and showed no signs of wrapping up. He liked it, but he wanted to hear something new.

Merry found himself thinking about Ariadne again. About that phone call. About how she had sounded scared. It still bothered him. What if she tried to call again while he was away?

He couldn't worry about it. He wasn't Ariadne's husband anymore. He wasn't part of her life anymore. The phone call had been a mistake. She'd hung up, ended it without an explanation.

He wondered if maybe he wasn't running away from

everything by taking this trip. Running away from the whole Ariadne thing. Running away from the dead end his life had become since the marriage broke up. Running away from that nut who tormented him on the phone.

Sometimes a man has to go away. He has to distance himself from all the bullshit and clear his head. Besides, he wasn't running away from *everything*.

Lilac was with him.

She woke up and pulled away from his shoulder. He stretched an arm around her.

"Where are we?" she asked.

"We're almost there," he said. "We'll be there in less than an hour. We're making great time. There's no traffic or anything, and we're just zooming by."

"Good," she said. "I hate long car rides. When I was a kid, I used to dread vacations. When my parents were together, they'd take us to these stupid tourist spots. We'd be driving forever. After they broke up, my mom and her latest boyfriend would do the same shit. It was awful. Sometimes I'd get that motion sickness and I'd throw up inside the car and get yelled at. It was just torture."

"I don't know," Merry said. "I never went through anything like that. I didn't travel much as a kid. And any long drives I did later, I did the driving. It doesn't seem so bad that way."

"I still hate it."

"What about planes?" Merry asked. "You take a lot of planes?"

"When I can. I don't mind that much. I kind of like planes. Taking off and landing, it's kind of fun. Not like a car. A car just drones on and on."

"I guess I kind of equate cars with freedom. Just hop in and go wherever you want."

"What's with the music?"

"It's jazz."

"I know that," Lilac said. "This song has been going on forever."

"You noticed that too, huh? Change the station if you want."

She fooled around with the tuner until she got a rock 'n' roll station. The Rolling Stones were doing *Satisfaction.*

He hadn't heard the song in a while, and it sounded better than he remembered.

"Here's our exit coming up. It won't be long now."

"Thank Jesus," Lilac said. "I just want to stretch my legs again."

"We're both tired, that's all. But I knew we could get there in a day, if we didn't stop along the way."

She was in a crabby mood, being tired and all. It had nothing to do with age, but her whining reminded him of how much younger she was, and it irritated him. On the few long trips he'd taken with Ariadne, she'd been silent the whole time. Suffering in silence.

"Are you going to tell your friend what I do for a living?" Lilac asked. "What you're going to do soon, too?"

"There's no reason to bring it up."

"I don't mind if you do," Lilac said. "It doesn't bother me. I'm not ashamed of it."

"Let's just forget about things and enjoy this little trip."

"You're still going to do that movie with me, right?"

"Sure. I told you I would, didn't I?"

"Because when I called Tony before we left, and told him, he was happy about your decision. He thinks it will be good."

"I know, I know. You already told me."

"I'm sorry I'm so boring."

"You're not boring. It's just been a long drive and we're both tired."

She wriggled in his grip. Then, "I just wanted to make sure you didn't change your mind, that's all."

"Don't worry about it."

"How long has that weird guy been calling you?" Lilac asked.

"Huh?"

"That weird guy who calls your place."

"Do we really have to talk about this? I was trying to forget about him."

"I was just wondering if it's been going on a long time."

"Not really. On and off for a couple of weeks."

"You said you went over there," Lilac said. "To scare him?"

"Yeah." The whole thing made him uneasy.

"Don't worry about it," he said. "I'll take care of it when we get back. He won't be calling anymore."

Lilac turned off the radio. "I'm starting to get a headache."

"Okay."

"And I really have to pee. Are we almost there?" Lilac sat up in the seat and looked around. They were off the highway now and in a residential area.

There were houses all around them.

"His street's just right up here. We're almost there."

"Good. Will your friend let us sleep in the same room?"

"Sure," Merry said. "Why the fuck not? We're adults."

"Some people are weird like that."

"We're all adults here. Stop worrying."

"When we fuck, do you want me to keep quiet?"

"Do what you want," Merry said, getting annoyed.

"Are we going to stay there the whole two weeks?"

"Listen, I'm starting to get a headache now, too. Can we just drive in silence until we get there?"

Lilac pulled away and pressed her head against the passenger side window.

He put both hands on the steering wheel.

It was their first fight.

CHAPTER 36

It was late when Ariadne got back to her apartment. She opened the door and stumbled in, exhausted from the flight. Mitch was behind her. They put their bags down in the hallway, and then Mitch stretched out on the couch.

"Do you want something to eat?" Ariadne asked. "I'm going to get some food."

"I just want to sleep," Mitch said.

"Well don't fall asleep there," Ariadne said. "Use the bed."

"Can you show me the way?" Mitch asked.

"Get up," Ariadne said. She didn't try to help him up. "You're a big boy now."

Mitch reluctantly stood and followed her to the bedroom.

"Just make yourself comfortable. I'll be right back."

"Hurry up," Mitch said. He started getting undressed.

"Do you have to call anyone now that we're back or anything?" Ariadne asked.

"No, it can wait until morning," Mitch said. He fumbled with his clothes and then stretched out on the bed. When they were on the plane, he'd told her he should probably go back to his place tonight and make some calls, but the flight was delayed. They got back much later than expected, and her place was closer to the airport. He just wanted to sleep.

She let him sleep.

Ariadne went to the kitchen and poured herself a glass of wine. She saw the machine blinking and listened to Francie's messages. Then she dialed her number.

"Hello?"

"Hi Francie, I just got back."

"Good to hear your voice. Did you enjoy the trip?"

"I had a great time. Did you get the postcards?"

"Yes, I did," Francie said. "Did it have something to do with work?"

"No, it was just a chance to get away from everything," Ariadne said. "I really needed that."

"Were you alone?" Francie asked.

Ariadne knew what Francie meant. Hell, she'd known about Francie's feelings for a long time. It had created a kind of sexual tension between them, which was kind of fun sometimes. They'd tease each other, flirt. Francie was a warm, attractive woman, and there were times when Ariadne really wondered what it would be like to be intimate with her. She found it almost odd that nothing had ever come of it, after all the years they had known each other.

But she had just never pursued it.

"Francie, I went with Mitch," Ariadne said. "That guy I told you about."

"Oh," Francie said, sounding disappointed. "Was it fun?"

"It was the best time I'd had in years," Ariadne said. "I felt so alive there. I really needed to get away."

"I'm glad you had fun," Francie said. "The postcard looked wonderful. Did you have nice weather?"

"It was perfect," Ariadne said. "How have you been doing?"

"I missed you," Francie said.

"I know," Ariadne said.

"Things have been okay, I guess. Same old, same old."

"Have you been drinking, Francie?" Ariadne asked.

"A little."

"You've been crying too, haven't you?"

"No," Francie said.

"You can be honest with me. You know that. We can tell each other anything."

"I love you, Ariadne."

"I know, Francie."

"No," Francie said. "I *love* you."

"I know. I've known for a long time now."

"You don't hate me?" She looked at the wine glass she was holding. Her speech was slurred. *She had probably been drinking for hours,* Ariadne thought. *Well, at least she wasn't drinking alone now.*

"No way. Not in the slightest."

"But you don't feel the same way."

"You really should get some sleep. It's pretty late."

Her voice was soft, gentle. "I'm sorry."

"For what? There's nothing for you to be sorry about. I'm the one who called."

"I'm probably drunk, and I laid this crap on you. I don't know why I do these things."

Because you've been holding a torch for me for years, Ariadne thought, *and it's taking its toll.*

"Go to sleep. Everything will be fine in the morning."

"Okay."

"Good night, Francie."

"Good night, Ariadne. Thanks for calling. It's really nice to hear your voice."

"We'll talk more tomorrow."

She finished her glass of wine, poured another, and went back to the bedroom.

Mitch was fast asleep, snoring. Ariadne covered him with a sheet. Then she left the room and closed the door. She wasn't really tired anymore.

She went back to the living room and turned on the TV. She flipped channels until she found an old Barbara Stanwyck movie she'd never seen before that looked interesting.

She hugged her legs on the couch and watched. The sound was low, so she had to strain to hear.

Every now and then, she took a sip of wine. When the glass was empty she refilled it.

She felt bad about the phone call with Francie. She felt guilty, even though she hadn't done anything wrong.

She fell asleep before the movie was over.

CHAPTER 37

"Merry, my man," Phil said, opening the door. "You made it!"

"Ahead of schedule," Merry said. He carried their bags in both hands as they walked up the driveway. "Long time no see, buddy."

Phil was a stocky guy with long brown hair. Lilac squeezed past him and went inside, making room for Merry to bring in the baggage. Phil just stood there, oblivious to the fact that if he just moved out of the way, it would be easier for everyone.

Lilac thought maybe he just stood there so she would brush up against him, but it was too early to make a judgment call like that, and she wanted to give a friend of Merry's the benefit of the doubt.

"Get out of the way, huh?" Merry said, struggling to get by.

"Sure thing," Phil said with a smirk.

He stepped aside, giving Merry a wide berth.

"Hi, I'm Erin," a woman's voice from the other room said.

She was slightly taller than Phil, and from the looks of her thin build but large bosom, chances were good she had been a recipient of breast implants.

"Hi, I'm Lilac."

"Hi," Erin said. "Hi, Merry. It's been a long time." She moved forward and hugged Merry.

"Sure has," Phil said. "I didn't know when I'd ever get to see you again, buddy."

"So, you see me now, right?"

"We have a room all ready for you two," Erin said. "We had no idea when you'd get here."

"Neither did we," Merry said. "But we hauled ass getting out here."

"You can put that stuff down, you know," Phil said to Merry.

"I thought maybe you'd show us to our room. You don't have much in the way of manners, do you?"

"Yeah, sure, this way," Phil said, pushing between Merry and Lilac and heading down the hall. Merry followed close behind. Lilac just stood there, watching them enter a room at the end of the hall.

There was an uncomfortable silence, and Lilac saw Erin looking at her, both of them unsure of what to say to break the tension.

"So, have you been going with Merry long?" Erin finally asked.

It had been less than three weeks. Lilac thought that sounded funny to say. She said, "A little while."

"Where did you guys meet?"

"I just happened to be in his neighborhood. And we kind of connected. It was kind of like fate, I guess."

"Pretty wild," Erin said. "Phil and I met kind of like that. I used to work the late shift at this twenty-four-hour store, and Phil used to come in every night and chew the fat. It was pretty cool, because this was real late, and either I was alone or there were like these creepy types hanging around. I was taking college courses, and I'd bring my books to work so I could read while it was slow, and Phil used to ask me all kinds of questions and stuff. So I really started looking forward to seeing him whenever I worked late, and when we decided to go on a real date, it seemed like totally natural, you know?"

Lilac smiled. "Sounds romantic," she said.

"It really was," Erin agreed.

"What courses were you taking?"

"I was going to go for a degree in business, but I sort of dropped out."

"I'm thinking of going back myself," Lilac said.

"Really?" Erin asked. "What for?"

"Art maybe."

Phil and Merry came back in.

"What are you two standing around for?" Phil asked, looking both women over. "Sit down and take a load off!"

"Where are my manners?" Erin asked. "Come this way." She led them into the living room, and everyone sat down.

"What do you like?" Phil said.

"Vodka rocks," Merry said.

"I got the good stuff," Phil said. "Straight from Russia. Just for you."

"Well, then, don't be stingy with it."

"How about you, Lily?" Phil asked.

"Lilac," she said. "I'll have a screwdriver."

"Sure thing." Phil went to the kitchen and came back with a carton of orange juice.

"I was just telling Lilac how we met," Erin said.

"Fascinating story," Phil said and laughed.

"I think it's nice," Erin said.

Phil poured the drinks and brought them over.

"So what are you doing these days?" Phil asked Merry.

"Nothing yet."

"Man, you'd better find something soon, before your mother's money runs out."

"Don't worry about me," Merry said. "I've got it all under control."

"Sure you do," Phil said. "Like when you quit the cops. That was a real smart move. What the hell else are you qualified for now? You could be a security guard, I guess."

"It's under control," Merry said again.

Lilac felt a tension between the two men, which made her wonder why Merry seemed to think Phil was such a good friend. They were practically antagonistic toward each other. It could have been good-natured ribbing, but she sensed an edge in there.

"You're not getting any younger," Phil said. "You just had a birthday, didn't you?"

"Yeah," Merry said. "I try not to think about it."

"Erin insisted we get you a cake or something, but I told her you wouldn't go for it."

"I can't imagine anyone who doesn't want to celebrate their birthday," Erin said.

Lilac thought back to the birthday cake she had shared with Merry in his apartment.

"So, did I mention yet that Erin here's expecting?"

"Oh, that's great," Lilac said

"Isn't it?" Erin asked. "We just found out. I'm about two months along. I can't wait."

"I'm surprised you and Ariadne never had any kids," Phil said. "It might have kept your marriage together."

Merry glared at him. It was obvious the mention of Ariadne bothered him.

"The marriage was doomed," Merry said. "Nothing would have saved it. And the reason we didn't have any kids is because we didn't want any."

"I can't imagine anyone not wanting kids," Erin said, truly perplexed. "Don't you want kids someday, Lilac?"

"I don't know," Lilac said. "I guess it's not something I think about much."

"Well you're still young yet," Erin said.

"Hey, Merry," Phil said. "What if Lilac here decides she wants kids? You planning to give her a hard time about it?"

Merry drained his glass. "We'll cross that bridge when we come to it. Besides, I don't think that has anything to do with you."

"Just asking," Phil said. "Just making conversation."

"Phil," Erin said. "Maybe this isn't the best topic."

"I just wanted to tell my buddy here that my wife's expecting a baby, that's all. What's so awful about wanting to share something so wonderful?"

"It's great news," Merry said, clearly trying to just end the whole line of questioning.

"Ain't it?" Phil asked. "You want a refill there, buddy?"

"Sure."

"How about you, Lilac? That's such a unique name."

She finished what was left of her drink. She couldn't drink it fast enough. "Sure."

"I wish I could drink, but I guess I should think of the baby," Erin said.

"I don't think it would matter much," Phil said, "if you want a drink or two. Hell, my mother drank all nine months."

"And look how you turned out," Merry said with a laugh.

"Well, you still got that wit of yours, huh?"

"You guys," Erin said. "Who would ever know you've been such good friends since high school?"

"We first met in junior high," Phil said. "Seventh grade. Miss Gerard's class. Right, Merry?"

"Yeah, sure."

"Merry was the biggest guy in the class, so I thought it might be a good idea to become his friend. I was this little runt, and I was sick of getting grief for it."

"You're still a runt," Merry said. "Things haven't changed much."

"Here's your drink, funny guy."

Merry took the glass and moved closer to Lilac on the couch.

"We've been married four years," Erin said to Lilac. "Actually, more like four and a half."

"Yeah," Phil said. "And we lived together for three years before that."

"I told Lilac all about how we met, in the store and all," Erin said.

"You said that already," Phil said. "It's not that exciting."

"You know," Merry said. "It's really late, and I'm dead tired from driving all the way here. I think maybe we should turn in."

"So soon?" Phil asked. "Hell, it's not that late. We have so much to catch up on."

"Can we do it tomorrow?" Merry asked. "I'm bushed."

"I guess so," Phil said. "If you're that tired."

"Thanks," Merry said. He stood up and put his empty glass on the coffee table. Lilac stood up too. "We'll just go to our room."

"I'll bet you're not *too* tired," Phil said. "That Lilac's some looker."

Everyone laughed. Some of the laughter was forced.

"Do you have everything you need?" Erin asked, getting to her feet as well. "Do you need anything?"

"I don't think so," Merry said.

"The bathroom is right next to your room," Erin said.

"Thanks," Lilac said.

She followed Merry as he went down the hall to the guest room.

When they closed the door and were alone, Merry spread out on the bed. "Man, am I tired."

"Me too," Lilac said, starting to get undressed.

"So what do you think of Phil and Erin?" Merry asked.

She wanted to say they got on her nerves, and that she felt uncomfortable here, but instead, she said, "They seem nice enough."

"Don't worry," Merry said. "They'll grow on you when you get to know them."

Lilac slid on to the bed beside him.

"Why don't you get out of those clothes?" she asked him.

"I will. I just wanted to take a breather first. I forgot how much driving can take out of you."

He closed his eyes, and Lilac knew he was going to fall asleep like that, with his clothes on, stretched out on top of the sheets. But she didn't wake him.

She got up to turn off the light, then she climbed back into bed.

She put her arms around him and closed her eyes.

CHAPTER 38

When Ariadne woke the next morning, Mitch was already gone. She was in her bed, and she half-remembered him picking her up off the couch and carrying her back in here, but it was a fuzzy memory. More like a dream.

She slid off the bed, padded to the kitchen, and poured herself a glass of orange juice.

The apartment was so quiet. She hadn't thought of it that way in such a long time. Normally it didn't bother her to be alone.

There was a note stuck to the fridge with magnets. It read, "Love you. I'll call you soon."

Looking at the note, Ariadne had mixed emotions. It had sounded nice when he said it during their vacation, but now that they were back home, it bothered her. She had never said she loved him, too, because she wasn't sure what she felt. It had been so long since she'd said that to anyone. Sure, she had enjoyed spending time with him. But she didn't know why she had suggested they move in together. It had seemed like a fun idea at the time, but now she dreaded having to follow up on it, the possibility of losing her own space. She would put it off as long as she could.

Sure, she wanted to be loved, just like anyone else did. It had been a long time since she and Merry had been together and happy. But she was no longer sure if she was capable of love.

Real love.

Ariadne leaned against the counter and stared at the note. *What should I do now?* she wondered.

What if he calls? If he went back to work, there might be

a chance of a job for her today. After two weeks, surely they would have need of her services. In fact, during the whole trip she hadn't kept in contact with her employers. But then again, Mitch was one of her employers. He was the one who usually kept her informed, let her know when they needed her, and since she was with him, she didn't think of asking him if it was okay to be away from the job for so long. Ariadne wasn't sure how she felt about that now.

Was their relationship going to complicate things at work? Would what she did for a living eventually sour things? Was he going to try to get her to stop what she did, get a normal job, or even give up working and start a family with him?

She took the note down from the fridge. She rolled it into a ball and threw it away. *How will things change?* she wondered. *How will the way we act around each other change, now that things between us have reached a different level?*

She got dressed and left the apartment. She did not take her beeper.

CHAPTER 39

Lilac finished showering and got dressed. When she went back to the bedroom, Merry was still asleep and didn't look like he was going to be stirring anytime soon. She sat at the foot of the bed, wondering what to do.

If Merry hadn't been there, she would have left. She didn't feel comfortable here, and she had barely slept at all. She felt like she didn't belong here. She'd known people like Phil and Erin all her life, but she had left all that behind. She had moved on.

Maybe she was judging them too soon.

But she didn't think so.

Lilac just sat there watching Merry sleep, wanting to wake him up but knowing she shouldn't. He had been so tired and needed the sleep. But she didn't have anything to do here with him asleep, and she didn't want to go outside. She didn't want to deal with them.

There was a knock at the door. Soft at first, and then a little louder. Lilac was afraid it would wake Merry, so she got up to answer it.

It was Erin.

"I was wondering if you wanted any breakfast," Erin said.

"Merry's still sleeping."

"Then come with me," Erin said. "Let him sleep."

"Okay," Lilac said, reluctantly following her out of the room and gently closing the door.

"He certainly was tired, wasn't he?"

"Sure looks that way."

They went to the kitchen. There was food cooking on the

stove. Phil didn't appear to be up yet, Lilac noticed with relief.

"What would you like to eat?" Erin asked. "I'll make whatever you want."

"I'll have some scrambled eggs," Lilac said. "If it's no trouble."

"No trouble at all. I like cooking. Really. I think maybe I should have gone to cooking school. I could have been a chef or something."

"Wouldn't that take the fun out of it? Doing it for a living?"

"Maybe," Erin said thoughtfully. "But I'd like to go to cooking school anyway. I could just cook for Phil, you know, make him these incredible meals."

"Yeah."

"You want ham or bacon with those eggs?"

"Doesn't matter."

"I was going to have bacon," Erin said.

"Sure."

She grabbed supplies out of the fridge. "I knew you were up. I heard the shower and all. And I figured I'd go get you. I hate to eat alone. Phil's already gone, and I'm all alone."

"Did he go to work?" It was a Monday morning, but she assumed that maybe Phil had taken some vacation time or something, to spend time with Merry.

"I don't know. He didn't tell me. He just got up at the crack of dawn and left. I'm not sure when he'll be back. He makes his own hours, you know? He's his own boss. He comes and goes when he likes."

"What kind of work does he do?"

"He's a salesman," Erin said. "Not a traveling salesman. He sells to places in the city. All kinds of things. He works for a few different companies, selling their stuff. I don't ask him much about it. He doesn't like to talk about his work much."

"So you just stay at home, huh?"

"Yep," Erin said. "Phil likes it that way, and I guess I do, too. Although I wouldn't mind taking those cooking classes. I don't know, I guess I never really did want to get my degree in business. It was just something to do. Since I've been with Phil, he's all I need. And he makes a good living too."

"You have a nice house," Lilac said.

"Thanks."

"So how long have you known Merry?"

"I don't know," Erin said. "Years. He and Phil go way back. We used to see him a couple of times a year, but it's been a while. I know it's rough with the distance and all. We visited them a few times, when he was still with Ariadne."

"The famous Ariadne," Lilac said. "What was *she* like?"

"It's hard to say. When I met her, I think things were already falling apart between them. She was kind of cold, you know? Serious. She and Phil kept taking snipes at one another. I don't think Phil liked her very much, but I'd never seen anything like it."

That was one reason to like Ariadne. Lilac didn't care much for Phil either.

"How did Merry react to that?"

"He tried to get them to knock it off. It was really strained. I didn't feel comfortable around her. Later on, after they separated and Merry came out to visit us by himself, it was a lot better. I think Merry's a real nice guy. He definitely could have done better than Ariadne." Erin said. "I mean, look, he found you."

Lilac smiled at the compliment. At last, she'd found a topic that kept her interested in what Erin had to say.

"Do you know why Merry broke up with her?"

"Phil says she used to be different. She used to be funny and all. I didn't see any of that. Phil said she changed. And I guess they just didn't have anything in common anymore."

Erin finished making Lilac's breakfast and dished it out.

She had been making toast while the eggs and bacon were cooking on the stove, and she had a complete meal ready all at once. Lilac hadn't even noticed all the work she was doing as they talked.

"Has Merry mentioned anything to you about Ariadne?" Erin asked. "Does he talk about her at all?"

"A little," Lilac said. "But I don't think he likes to talk about her very much."

"Well, from what I saw, I think his breaking up with

Ariadne was the best thing Merry could have done. Now eat up before it gets cold."

"Thanks," Lilac said. It all looked so good.

Erin had been cooking her own food too, and dished it out as Lilac dug in. Erin sat across the table from Lilac.

"Do you need anything?" Erin asked. "Jam or anything?"

"No, everything's perfect," Lilac said.

"I'm so glad you carne out here," Erin said. "Sometimes it gets pretty lonely. It's nice to have another woman to talk to, you know?"

"Yeah," Lilac said.

"I mean, we have friends and all, but during the day, when Phil's gone, it's kind of quiet around here. *Too* quiet."

Lilac smiled and then ate a forkful of eggs.

"Do you work at all?"

Lilac thought about it. "I guess I'm kind of in movies."

"Movies!" Erin said. "Oh my God! That's incredible. What were you in? Anything I might have seen?"

"Just a couple of B-movies," Lilac said. "You know, trashy horror movie kind of things. Nothing all that great. No really big roles. Even if you saw one of them, you wouldn't notice me."

"I can't believe it! Movies!" Erin said, still very impressed. "We're going to have to rent one of them tonight. I just have to see you acting."

"I doubt if you can find any of them," Lilac said. "I don't think they'd have them in video stores or anything."

"Well, it wouldn't hurt to look. There's a video store close by and they have a really good selection."

Lilac realized she should have lied better. She should have said she worked in a store or something. But even though most people were kind of uptight about the kind of movies she *really* did, Lilac thought it was kind of cool that she was in movies, and she wanted to talk about it. The only thing was, she wasn't sure how people like Erin and Phil would react, and she didn't want to make things uncomfortable for Merry.

"We'll have to go to the video store later," Erin said. "Don't let me forget."

"I really doubt we'll find any of them. They were really small, low-budget things."

Erin wasn't hearing any of it. "Were they the kind of movies where this guy in a mask goes around killing people? Were you one of the victims?"

"Kind of," Lilac said.

"Phil and I watch movies like that sometimes," Erin said. "Phil just loves horror movies."

Lilac continued eating.

"They aren't some of those really bloody movies, are they?" Erin asked. "The really gross ones?"

"Yeah, they are," Lilac said. "Some of them are pretty gross."

"How can you do movies like that? Doesn't it bother you?"

"Nah, it's all fake. It's kind of fun, really."

"I don't know," Erin said. "Phil likes some of those, but they bother me. I mean, what if kids see them, you know? I've got to think about stuff like that, now that I have a baby coming. Phil won't be watching any more of those types of movies when the baby's here."

"I really don't think you'd like the kinds of movies I've done," Lilac said, wanting badly to change the subject. "They're pretty bad."

"You're probably right," Erin said. "But I want to see one anyway. I want to see you acting. I can fast forward it if it gets too bloody."

Lilac looked down at her plate and continued eating.

"How long have you been acting in movies?" Erin asked. "Do you do a lot of them?"

It was obvious Lilac had opened a can of worms. Erin was hooked on the whole movie thing and wasn't about to let go of it all that easily.

"I've been doing it about two years now," Lilac said. "I guess I make about four or five movies a year."

"That's wonderful!" Erin said. "Do you think you'll ever go out to Hollywood and become a big star?"

"I doubt it," Lilac said. "I don't think I'm good enough for that."

"I'll be the judge of that," Erin said. "We really have to rent one of your movies today."

Lilac was just about finished eating. She had no idea how she was going to get away from Erin and all this talk about movies. She thought maybe she could say that she wanted to go for a walk, but then Erin would probably want to come along too. She might even suggest they walk to a video store. It made sense; people were usually interested in things like movies. Lilac really should have thought of a better lie before she spoke.

At that moment, Merry came in. He wiped the sleep from his eyes. He was still in the same clothes he'd been wearing the night before. Lilac had tried to get them off him, but he was too heavy and was sleeping too deeply.

"Good morning, Merry," Erin said, noticing his entrance first. "Would you like some breakfast?"

"Sure," Merry said. "Maybe I should take a shower first, huh?"

"Don't be silly," Erin said. "It's only us here. You must be starving. I'll make you something right away."

Merry looked at Lilac and grimaced, and then he sat at the table. "Hope I don't smell too bad," he whispered to Lilac.

"Like she said, it's just us here," Lilac said. "Don't worry so much. It's too late to worry about first impressions." She winked at him.

"So, Merry," Erin said, standing at the stove with her back to them. "You didn't tell us Lilac's in the movies!"

Lilac could have seen the shock on Merry's face a mile away.

CHAPTER 40

When Ariadne got back to her place, after shopping most of the day with Francie, the light on the answering machine was flashing, and she knew who it was before she played the message. She didn't even listen to it before she dialed his number.

"That you, Mitch?"

"Ariadne, where the hell have you been?"

"Out. Getting some air."

"You'd better get ready pretty quick," Mitch said. "You've got a job. I left a few messages on your machine after you wouldn't answer your beeper. You didn't even have it on, did you?"

"I forgot to bring it."

"Jesus, Ari. I thought you'd never get back to me."

Ariadne rolled her eyes and looked at Francie, who had put her bags down and was sitting on the couch.

"Can't you find someone else?" Ariadne asked. "I'm with my friend Francie. She took the day off work, so we could spend some time together."

"Ariadne, this is serious," Mitch said. "You need to get ready and get down here."

Ariadne wished she hadn't called.

"I don't know," she said.

"Look," Mitch said, getting annoyed. "We took two weeks off. Vacation's over. I need you here *now*."

"Mitch, I've been thinking about the job," Ariadne said. "I don't know if I want to do this anymore. I need some time to think about it."

"This is the wrong time for this. What happened to the girl

who told me this job was part of who you are, that it was in your blood? Now all of a sudden you do this about-face. You're really putting me in a spot here."

Ariadne covered the phone. "Francie, I have to go to work."

"Well, we had a pretty good day while it lasted," Francie said.

"Ariadne, you there?"

"Yes, Mitch, I'm here."

"So what is it?"

"I'm getting ready. I'll be there. Same place as before?"

"No, not this time. I'll send a car to get you. Be downstairs in about half an hour. No later. Okay?"

"Okay."

"Don't let me down, Ariadne. I'm in a real bind. I need you down here as soon as possible. I'm not kidding."

"I'll be there."

"Great," Mitch said. "Love you, babe. I knew you wouldn't let me down."

"Uh, huh."

"Don't forget, the car will be there in half an hour."

"I'll be ready."

Ariadne hung up. She turned to Francie. "I'm really sorry about this. He sounded desperate."

"Were you serious about that? About not wanting to do that kind of work anymore?"

"I don't know. It had been so long since I had a break. A real break; time to relax and think about things. I think I'm getting sick of being on call all the time, and having to drop everything whenever Mitch or one of those guys calls me."

"You sure that your work isn't starting to bother you? Not even a little bit?"

"I don't know. Maybe, sometimes." Ariadne thought of Fredericks showing up at her door. It shook her up more than she thought.

"I've got to get ready," Ariadne said. "A car's corning for me."

"I'll be going," Francie said. "I really had a great time today, shopping and all. I'm glad I took the day off. It was a lot of fun."

"Yeah, it was. We have to do it again sometime."

"You bet."

"Things might be kind of weird for a while," Ariadne said. "I really don't know what's going to happen between Mitch and me. I need some time to work it out."

"Take as much time as you need."

"Thanks. I'll call you soon. I promise."

"I know you will."

"I'll call you a taxi."

Ariadne picked up the phone and ordered a cab. Francie stood, gathering her shopping bags.

"Okay, you're all set. It should be here any minute."

"Thanks," Francie said, standing near the door.

"I'm really sorry about this."

"Don't worry about it."

"I wish I could play hooky sometimes. I mean, I guess I did, when I went off with Mitch and all. But that was different. I'd just like to be able to say no once in a while."

CHAPTER 41

"Something's been bugging me," Phil said. "And I really don't know how to say it."

"What?" Merry asked.

Phil had insisted Merry go with him for a walk. Now he stopped and shook his head.

"Hell, I don't know."

"Come on," Merry said. "Just say it already."

"I've seen your girlfriend before," Phil said.

Merry tensed. He knew what was coming next. He just didn't know how to play it.

"What do you mean?"

"I've seen her, man," Phil said.

Merry didn't say anything.

"In movies," Phil said. "*Porno* movies. There, I said it."

"I know," Merry said.

"You know?" Phil said.

Merry shrugged.

"And it doesn't bother you?" Phil asked. "How did you meet a girl like that, anyway?"

"She was in my neighborhood. It was kind of funny. We just met. I asked her to lunch."

"You just went up to her and asked her?"

"Yep."

"And just like that, you got her in the sack?"

"No," Merry said. "She came over to my place, and we ate lunch. We talked."

"You didn't fuck that first time?" Phil asked. "A girl like that? I find that hard to believe."

Merry was feeling uncomfortable. He hesitated.

"Isn't she a little young?" Phil asked.

"What's with all the questions?" Merry asked.

"I mean, what is she? Eighteen?"

"She's twenty-one."

"Did you ask to see some ID?"

"Give me a break, man."

"Aren't you afraid of getting diseases?"

"She gets tested regularly," Merry said. "She's clean."

"How can you ever be sure?" Phil said. "Someone who makes a living like that?"

"Don't worry about it."

"Look, I'm not trying to give you a hard time," Phil said. "It's just that I worry about you sometimes, Merry. Ever since you quit the force, I've been really scared that you're screwing up big time."

"I don't need you to plan my life for me," Merry said. "I think I can handle it."

"Are you sure about that?"

"Fuck you," Merry said, half-jokingly.

"So what's it like?" Phil asked, suddenly changing his tone. He dug at Merry with his elbow. "She must know some wild stuff, doing that for a living."

"She's great," Merry said. "Absolutely great."

"I figured as much," Phil said, smiling. "I'm jealous, man. Really."

"Erin's as beautiful as ever," Merry said.

"I know," Phil said. "But that doesn't stop a man from looking, or from craving variety once in a while."

"I know what you think about Lilac," Merry said. "But it's not some kind of mindless sex bullshit. I mean, we talk. We really talk. It's more than just that. We've got a real connection."

"Are you sure you can have a real relationship with someone like that?" Phil asked. "Are you sure you can live with her, knowing she fucks other guys for a living? I've seen her movies, pal, and she looks like she really digs it."

"How many movies have you seen?"

"With her? About five or six, maybe. She's hot. Going to be big, maybe."

"You sound like you know a lot about it."

"I like movies. I like watching that stuff. Don't tell me you don't."

"I guess I don't watch as much as you."

"You always were kind of uptight about some things," Phil said.

Merry ran a hand through his hair. He was starting to get pretty thin on top. Maybe he *was* too old for her. "We should head back. Dinner's probably ready."

"Yeah, we can head back. I just wanted some time to talk to you alone," Phil said. "Relax. I'm just curious, that's all. You know, I really am glad you came for a visit. We haven't been able to talk one on one like this for a long time. I miss it, I really do. Remember when we were kids, all we did was talk?"

"I remember."

"We talked about all kind of shit. Comic books. Monster movies. Stupid shit. What we wanted to do with our lives. Where we'd be when we got out of school. All that bullshit."

"Yeah."

"And we talked about girls. All the time. Man, the lack of pussy made us think about it all the time. Remember? Now we're all set. We've got it. And we still talk about it."

"*You're* doing most of the talking."

"Bullshit," Phil said with another smile.

Merry smiled too.

"We're like a couple of kids, even now."

"Where we are, now that we're out of school and we're grown up and all," Merry said. "Is it what you thought it would be?"

"I don't know," Phil said. "I'm pretty happy. I've got a great wife. My job's going pretty well. I'm good at it. I make good money. I've got a house, two cars. I've got the American dream, buddy. There's not a lot I can complain about."

"Look at me," Merry said. "I don't know what the fuck I want to do with my life. I'm at this impasse, man. I'm at this fork in the road, and I don't know which way to turn."

"You'll figure it out," Phil said. "You always did before. Why should it change now? I didn't mean to upset you, man.

You know what I think messed you up? That Ariadne bitch. I don't know what it is she did to you to put you in a tailspin, but you've been chasing your own tail ever since."

"I really don't want to talk about Ariadne, Phil."

"You *never* want to talk about her," Phil said. "Sometimes I lay awake at night, wondering what it was that broke up your marriage. I mean, did you catch her doing it with another guy or what?"

"I told you to drop it," Merry said.

"Okay, I'll drop it," Phil said, seeing that Merry meant it. "But you better get your head together, soon. Stop going in circles. Your marriage has been over for a while now, it's time to pick up the pieces, Merry, and get on with your life."

"I am getting on with it," Merry said. "I'm doing fine."

"Do you have a job yet?"

"I'm going to be starting one," Merry said. "Soon enough."

"What kind of job?"

"You'll see," Merry said.

"Come on, tell me," Phil said. "I can't wait to hear it."

Merry stared at the darkening sky.

"You don't have a job lined up, do you?"

"I'm going to be in movies."

"Bullshit."

"Believe what you want."

Phil looked at his friend, apparently trying to figure him out. "You mean one of *those* movies? The kind *she* makes?"

"Maybe."

"You've got to be out of your fucking mind," Phil said. "What with all the diseases these days and all. What are you, a nut? And what would they want with a guy your age? They've got young studs for those roles."

"I've got a dick, don't I?" Merry asked.

"Is it big enough for *those* kinds of movies, Merry?"

"Lilac seems to think so. And I'm in pretty good shape for a guy my age. I work out. I keep in shape, probably better than a lot of those young guys."

"So you gonna fuck all kinds of women on camera?" Phil asked with a grin.

"No, I don't think so," Merry said. "Just Lilac."

"Man, you've got some crazy life. The more you talk, the crazier it all sounds. Here I am, living this peaceful, secure life and you're having a fucking adventure. I have to admit, sometimes I really am jealous. No matter how fucking nuts you sound."

As they approached the house, they saw that Erin was standing on the front steps. "There you guys are. Dinner's ready!"

"Do me a favor. Don't talk about any of this in front of Lilac," Merry said. "I don't want to embarrass her."

"Embarrass her?" Phil said. "When I got in the door, the first thing Erin tells me is that Lilac told her she's actress, that she's in these horror movies and we have to rent one right away."

"I know," Merry said. "I know."

"How long does Lilac think it'll take before we catch on?"

"I don't know. I really don't think she cares, though. Not really. I mean, she's not ashamed of what she does."

"I don't doubt it."

"Just don't bring it up, okay?" Merry said. "I mean, if she brings it up herself, fine, but don't do it for her."

"Whatever," Phil said. "So what did you do all day while I was at work? You and your girlfriend didn't make any movies with my wife, did you?"

Phil laughed. Merry laughed too.

"If you ever do anything like that, make sure I'm in on it too," Phil said, and he sounded like he meant it.

"Let's just go inside," Merry said. "I'm suddenly very hungry."

CHAPTER 42

"Jack?"

"Yeah, it's me."

"I wasn't sure you were there."

"I was out running," Jack said, breathing hard. "What is it?"

"You sure you're not fucking someone?" Tony asked. "That's what it sounds like to me."

"Yeah," Jack said. "That's my idea of exercise, all right!"

They both laughed.

"We're shooting a new flick in a week and a half," Tony said. "You want in?"

"Sure," Jack Underwood said. "I could use the money."

"Great," Tony said.

"So who am I working with?"

"That's what I wanted to talk to you about," Tony said. "Are you sure this is a good time?"

"No problem," Jack said. "I can fuck and chew gum at the same time."

They both laughed again.

"So who's in the cast?"

"Well, I've got Heather for the female lead," Tony said. "You'll be doing a scene with her and someone else. Maybe Chrissie."

"Chrissie?" Tony said. "I'm starting to feel like I'm married to that bitch. What about Lilac, is she in it?"

"Yeah," Tony said. "But she has only one scene with a guy, and it's already set up."

"Who is it?"

"That new boyfriend of hers."

"Merry?" Underwood said, laughing. "You've got to be fucking kidding me. Did you make him audition, see what he's packing?"

"Not yet," Tony said, "but from what Lilac told me, I think he'll be fine.. As long as he can work with an audience. He seems pretty game. Some of the best scenes I've ever filmed have been people in real relationships, you know. And Lilac hasn't done a boy-girl scene in a long time. I figured this was the only way I could get her to do it."

"Well, if he can't work it out, I'll fill in for him!"

They both laughed again.

"Sounds good," Underwood said. "Count me in. Where's filming going to be?"

"I've got this buddy who is a caretaker in Florida," Tony said. "Every year, he takes care of a different house. He's cool about the whole movie thing. Really cool. These are rich people's houses; he watches them while they take trips around the world or whatever shit. Well, he calls me and tells me he has this house right now; it's a fucking mansion. With crystal chandeliers, a kidney-shaped swimming pool, the works. So I'm thinking of rounding up a bunch of people, making two or three movies there at once. There's like a fifty rooms or something. It'll be incredible."

"Sounds good."

"Just do me one favor, okay?"

"Anything."

"I don't know what's going on between you and that Merry guy, but play it cool, okay? I don't want any fights breaking out on the set. Especially since I don't have insurance if anything in that house gets broken."

"I'll be cool," Underwood said. "Cool as a fucking cucumber. A fucking foot-long cucumber."

They both laughed.

"Well, I got to go now, I'm about to come," Underwood said. "So call me back when you got the details."

"Sure thing," Tony said, and hung up.

Jack went back into the bedroom, where a woman was squirming on the bed. He had tied her up pretty good. She was a bartender he had met the night before. They'd flirted a little and then he'd left. He met her after hours, when she was locking up. No one was around. She seemed more than interested, so he suggested they go to another bar for drinks, since she hadn't been allowed to drink while she was working. She agreed. They went someplace where no one knew either of them. Had some drinks. Then he brought her back to his place. They'd been fucking all night long.

She was really kind of cute.

He couldn't wait to get back into bed with her, and put his hands around that cute little neck of hers.

She screamed beneath the duct tape, but it was muffled. He told her not to struggle too much. The ropes would dig into her skin if she did. But she didn't listen. They never did.

CHAPTER 43

They were in the video store, looking in the horror section for one of Lilac's movies, and not having any luck.

"There just aren't any here," Lilac said, winking at Merry, who was starting to look uncomfortable.

"You didn't tell me any titles," Erin said. "Tell me some. Maybe *I'll* find one."

"It's no use," Lilac said. "This place isn't very well stocked."

"I don't know about that," Phil said.

Lilac shot him a dirty look. Merry had told her, before they left the house, that Phil knew the truth about her movie career.

If she'd had any brains, Lilac would have told Erin the truth right then and there, instead of going along on this wild goose chase. But she had resisted for some reason. The fact was, she and Erin had finally started to bond, and Lilac didn't want to lose that so quickly by letting her in on the truth.

Now that they were in the video store, Lilac felt like an absolute fool. "It's no use," she said again. "None of them are here."

"We can't give up that easily," Erin said, going over to the counter.

"I don't like my wife being made a fool of," Phil said, moving in close to Lilac and Merry. "If one of you doesn't tell her the truth, I will."

"Okay, okay," Lilac said, feeling like the fool herself. "I should never have said anything about movies."

"Too late now," Phil said.

Lilac walked over to Erin.

"Here she is," Erin said to the man behind the counter. "My

friend here is a real live movie actress, but we can't seem to find any of her videos. Why don't you tell him some of the names of your movies, Lilac?"

Lilac looked at the guy.

The smirk on his face told her he had seen her work. "Yeah," he said. "Tell me some names."

"Erin," Lilac said. "I think I found one."

"I might have a few back here," the guy behind the counter said, jerking his thumb in the direction of the adult section.

Lilac forced a laugh and grabbed Erin's arm, leading her back to the horror section. "Erin," she said, when they were alone. "I have something to confess."

"Oh?" She looked annoyed and stood very still.

"I never made any horror movies," Lilac said, and was going to leave it at that, making it sound like she just lied about the whole thing, but she knew Phil would say something to her later, and it was better to just come clean.

"What do you mean?"

"I guess I'm kind of an actress, but not the B-movie kind. I've made a few movies, but they're more like the dirty kind."

"Porno?"

"Yeah," Lilac said. "I didn't know how to say it before. I'm sorry I lied to you."

"You really do that for a living?"

Lilac couldn't really read her reaction. "Yeah."

"I don't normally look at those kinds of things," Erin said. "Although I know Phil likes them."

"I guess I was kind of afraid to tell you. I didn't know what you'd think of me."

"Do you mind if we rent one of your movies?" Erin asked. "One of your *real* movies?"

"Are you sure?"

"I'm so curious," Erin asked. "Will it make you feel uncomfortable?"

Lilac thought about it. Now that Erin knew, she would rent something eventually anyway, and Lilac would stay in suspense, wondering what Erin's reaction would be. This way, the suspense would be over. She'd know Erin's reaction once and for all. And the air would be clear. Besides, she'd never really watched one of her own movies with an audience before. It would be a new experience.

Phil and Merry came over. They had found a couple of videos they wanted to see.

"I told her," Lilac said.

"What, everyone knew but me?" Erin said. "Thanks for letting me in on it, Phil."

"I was going to tell you eventually. I was going to wait until they left."

"I want to rent one of her movies," Erin said.

"You sure about that?" Phil asked.

"It's okay with me," Lilac said. "What do you feel about it, Merry?"

"Yeah, Merry?" Phil said with a grin. "What do you feel about it?"

Merry looked like he would run out the door at any minute. "It's up to Lilac. If she's okay with it, so am I."

"That's pretty big of you," Phil said. "I don't know if I'd be so cool about it."

They walked over to the adult section.

"Which one should we get?" Erin asked.

"I kind of like this one," Phil said, pointing it out.

"That one's pretty good," Lilac said.

Merry said nothing.

Phil grabbed the empty video case, and they all walked toward the counter.

"We'll take these," Phil said, putting the cases down on the counter and taking out his rental card.

"So we've got a genuine celebrity in the store today," the guy behind the counter said.

Merry shot him an angry look. The guy frowned.

"I was just going to ask for an autograph."

"Sure," Lilac said, smiling. It had only happened a couple of times before, and never in front of other people she knew. It made her feel kind of special.

She borrowed the guy's pen and signed the back of an advertisement flyer on the counter.

"Thanks a lot," the guy said, ringing up the order. "My boss won't believe me."

Lilac felt so good at the moment, it was a kind of high, that all the discomfort she'd had over revealing her secret had washed away. She felt the way she thought real Hollywood stars did, getting recognized, signing autographs.

Merry was quiet as they left the store. Lilac had put him in a tough situation. He would have to sit in front of the television, watching his girlfriend having sex with strangers, while Phil and Erin watched along. She wished she had never mentioned movies. But it didn't matter now. Besides, Phil knew anyway. It wouldn't have remained a secret for long.

Phil started the car. "Maybe we should pick up some popcorn and refreshments on the way home."

Everyone laughed, except Merry, who just grunted, staring at the sign outside a tanning salon.

CHAPTER 44

The car arrived precisely thirty minutes later and took Ariadne to a place she'd never been before, a three-story brownstone on the outskirts of the city. The chauffer opened the car door and led her up the stairs.

He rang the doorbell three times when a man dressed in a tuxedo opened the door and looked at Ariadne with mock surprise.

"Oh, how nice to see you again," he said, though they had never met. "Please come in. The party's just started."

Her driver left. She went inside feeling uncomfortable about the whole set up.

The tuxedoed man led her through a crowd of partygoers, up a long flight of stairs to the second floor.

A few people were milling around.

"You must be Ariadne," the man said, when they had a little more privacy.

"Yes." She didn't ask his name.

"I'm Reynold," he said, telling her anyway. "Mitch told me about you. Said you were the best."

"Where's Mitch?" she asked. "Is he here?"

"I'm sorry. He had business elsewhere. Everything's been arranged though. The third floor is mostly soundproofed, and the party downstairs should cover any snippets of noise that might get through."

"I see."

"Follow me," Reynold said, going up another flight of stairs.

At the top of these stairs a large man in a suit waited for them.

"She's here," Reynold said to the man, who stepped aside to let them pass.

Ariadne had never been in this place before, had never seen these people before. It wasn't all that strange to work in a new place, but she had worked with Mitch directly for so long that it distressed her a little that he wasn't here.

Especially since she had so much to talk to Mitch about, and she suddenly found herself wanting very badly to see him again.

Reynold opened a door off the hallway and led her inside.

There was a man locked in a small cage that was just big enough to hold him. He didn't have much room to move—he certainly could not change his position-but he was facing her. He could just barely lift his head to look up at her.

There were also two burly men off to the side, in case they were needed.

Ariadne knew she had seen the man in the cage before. It was one of the men she had seen at the hotel, the last time she'd done a job for Mitch. One of Mitch's associates.

Now he was just another prisoner.

His eyes grew wide when he saw her. He'd seen her work, and he knew what was in store.

She pretended not to recognize him. She didn't know what the game was and didn't want to put herself at a disadvantage.

"I have some questions for this man," Reynold said. "And I want you to make him talk."

"I can do that."

"Good," Reynold said. "Mitch said you were the best. I respect his judgment."

"Thank you."

"You have quite a reputation, Ariadne," Reynold said. "May I call you by your first name?"

"Of course," she said. Then added, "Reynold."

"Yes, let's be on a first-name basis," Reynold said. "I'd like that."

"Will Mitch be coming shortly?"

"I'm sorry," Reynold said. "But like I said before, he's busy somewhere else right now. I don't expect him to be joining us this evening. I know he's your normal liaison in these matters, but he asked me to take care of it this time, and I hope this isn't a problem for you."

"No, not at all."

"Good. I thought Mitch might explain all this when he called you, but I guess he's just been so busy lately, since he got back from vacation. It must have slipped his mind."

Ariadne gave him a courtesy smile and then placed her case on the only table in the room. She started opening the locks.

"Oh, yes," Reynold said. "Let's start immediately."

She looked over her instruments, and then she looked over at the man in the cage.

"Are you going to tell us everything?" Reynold said. "Or do things have to get messy?"

Reynold crouched down beside the cage and stared at the man inside.

"Well?"

The man looked horrified, but didn't say anything.

"Still refuse to talk, huh?"

Reynold turned to face Ariadne.

"He's going to be a stubborn one, I'm afraid. Give him your worst. No one will hear him scream."

"I need access to his body parts," she said. "Can you take him out of the cage?"

"Certainly," Reynold said, nodding to the silent men who stood against the wall. One of them stepped forward and opened the cage door, and the other one reached in and grabbed the man harshly, yanking him out.

They made him stand. There was pain in his face, and Ariadne wondered how long he had been in the cage. The men then forced him over to a chair that was bolted to the floor. They sat him down and bound him securely with wire.

"Much better," Ariadne said.

"You may go," Reynold said to the men. "We'll call you if we require more assistance."

The men left without a word.

There was another wooden chair in the room, and Reynold dragged it to the back of the room. He sat on it backwards, watching. "I want you to hurt him. Don't worry about leaving any marks. I'll tell you when to stop. He won't answer anything until he realizes first that we mean business."

Reynold acted like a spectator at a boxing match. Like a voyeur at an orgy. He was really going to enjoy it, that much was apparent.

She took a scalpel out of her case and approached the man in the chair. She sliced away his clothes as he sat there, staring up at her without a sound.

When there was enough skin exposed, she went back to her bag of tricks and got out some long, silver needles.

The man in the chair grunted, but it didn't sound like words.

She looked behind her. Reynold was watching her work with rapt attention. He was definitely enjoying this.

CHAPTER 45

They all sat in the living room watching the big-screen TV. Merry, Lilac, and Erin sat on the couch while Phil sat on the reclining chair. They were all drinking beer and eating popcorn.

The movie was *Nuns in Heat*. It had been Lilac's third movie, if memory served her right. She played a young novice at a rather naughty convent. Her love scene with Freddy Tome had just ended. He'd played a visiting priest she had to show some hospitality to. In a short time, it would be the big lesbian orgy scene, where all the other nuns got a crack at her.

It had actually been kind of fun making it.

But sitting here, watching it, Lilac had mixed emotions about the whole thing. She had no idea what Erin thought—she just sat there, staring at the screen without making a sound. Merry wasn't much better. He was leaning back on the couch with an arm around Lilac, but he was pretty tense. His arm felt rigid behind her back.

It was no mystery what Phil's reaction was. Now and then, he'd say to Erin, "Come over here and sit with me," but she'd put him off, saying, "I'm trying to watch the movie."

When the orgy scene started, Lilac found herself watching Erin for a reaction, but she couldn't read the woman's face. It might have been disgust. It might have been interest. It was hard to say.

Lilac looked at Merry, sitting between them, and he just stared at the screen. His arm was stiff as a board behind her neck.

This was a really bad idea, Lilac thought.

"Come on, Erin," Phil said. "Come sit with me."

"Let me watch this."

"You can see it just as well from here."

"Shhh!"

"That's some acting there, Lilac," Phil said, and then laughed.

"Shhh!" Erin said again.

Lilac hadn't even thought of the whole religious thing when she'd picked it, that it might offend them. She wasn't religious and didn't really think about those things too often. It didn't seem to be a problem, though. Otherwise they probably would have shut it off by now.

The room was silent, except for the sounds from the TV, and after the orgy finale, the movie was over.

Phil pointed the remote and shut the VCR off.

"Well, that was it," Lilac said, feeling like she'd just come back from another planet.

"Man!" Phil said. "That was a wild one!"

Merry cleared his throat and squirmed in his seat.

"Wow, that was really you," Erin said, turning to look at Lilac. "I can't believe you did all that. I could never have done anything like that."

"You'd better not," Phil said.

"I mean even back when I was single. No way could I have done any of that. And on camera yet! Whoa!"

Lilac squirmed. Merry pulled his arm away.

"It's getting late," Phil said. "Maybe we should all get some sleep, huh?"

He got up from his chair and walked over to the TV. He ejected the videotape and turned on the news.

"How did you do those scenes with those women?" Erin asked, genuinely intrigued. "How did you keep from throwing up?"

"It's not so bad," Lilac said. "I mean, I don't consider myself a lesbian or anything. But it's not all that awful, once you do it a few times. I mean, I kind of like it better than scenes with men, you know?"

"Really?" Erin said. "I'd think a man would be better."

"When you do a scene with a guy, everything revolves

around him, and his keeping it up, you know? Sometimes a guy can hold things up for a while. And a lot of them can be creeps. The women are usually pretty nice."

"Don't you worry about disease and stuff?" Erin asked.

Lilac winced. Everyone who found out what she did asked her about that. It had almost driven a wedge between her and Merry, after all. "That's all strictly monitored. We all have to get tested regularly. It's a pretty controlled environment."

"But without condoms or anything, there's always a risk, isn't there?"

Life's a risk, Lilac thought, but she didn't say it. She said, "The risk's pretty low, from what I've seen. I've never heard of anyone I've known come down with anything too bad. And I know a lot of people in the business."

"We really should get to sleep," Phil said to Erin. "I've got to see some clients tomorrow, bright and early."

"Sure, Phil," Erin said.

"I hope the movie didn't freak you out too much, Erin," Lilac said. "I'm really sorry the whole thing came up at all. If I'd only said I was a secretary or something."

"Don't worry about it," Erin said. "I don't normally watch those kinds of movies, but this one was kind of fascinating. To think that I actually know someone who does that for a living."

"Besides, she would have found out anyway," Phil said. "I knew who you were the moment I first saw you."

Merry stretched. "Phil's right. It is kind of late."

"I hope it didn't embarrass you, all of us watching it?" Erin said. "I mean, it's one thing to act in one of those, but to watch it, watch yourself doing those things, it must feel funny."

It actually did, but Lilac didn't want to admit it. "No, I wasn't all that embarrassed," Lilac said.

"How about you, Merry?" Erin asked.

Merry grunted. "It was kind of strange, I guess."

"Do you still make those movies?" Erin asked.

"Yes."

"From what I hear, Merry's thinking about trying it himself," Phil said.

"Is that true?" Erin asked. She seemed shocked.

Merry shot Phil an angry look. "I don't know."

Lilac finished her beer. "Erin, I'll help you clean up here, okay?"

Erin hesitated, like she didn't want guests doing any of the work, but then she said, "Okay. Can you gather up the bottles?"

"Sure."

The women gathered up the empty bottles and popcorn bowls.

When the women were in the kitchen, Phil looked over at Merry. "Man, that's some hot chick you've got there!" Phil said. "I'd be afraid to get all burned up."

Merry scowled and got to his feet. "I'm pretty tired," he said. "I'm turning in."

"Don't go to bed mad," Phil called after him.

CHAPTER 46

It had been a very strange session, and not just because she had no clue where Mitch was. Who was this Reynold guy? She had never met him before, and took an instant dislike to him, but he seemed to know all about her. And who was the guy she was interrogating tonight? He had been one of the men shouting at the hotel, one of Mitch's men, but now he was on the receiving end of the knife. What did he do that changed his situation? And was something similar going to happen to Mitch?

Too many questions that didn't have answers. And there was no way she was going to ask Reynold anything. She didn't trust that man.

He had waited until the prisoner was almost dead until he told her the truth. That the man's tongue had been cut out before she even got there. There was no way he could talk, even if he wanted to. But then again, that didn't seem to be the point.

After a few hours, Reynold got bored and grabbed one of her scalpels. He slit the man's throat, ending the session.

She told him she didn't like anyone touching her instruments. Reynold apologized and told her she could go.

She felt nervous as she gathered her things, which was unusual for her. She almost thought that Reynold might prevent her from leaving, but he didn't. One of his guys showed up to escort her out. She didn't even ask if she could take a shower there. She could wait until she got home to clean up.

The car was waiting for her outside, and it drove her home. The driver didn't say a word during the drive back, and for that she was grateful.

Once home, she stripped and took a long shower. Then she

got into bed.

She had tried to call Mitch, but she kept getting his answering machine, and she didn't know any other way to reach him.

CHAPTER 47

Erin was singing.

It wasn't hard to figure out why. Lilac had heard their noises during the night and figured the movie had gotten their fires burning. But Merry hadn't been in the mood, rolled over in bed with his back to her. She had tried to talk to him about it, but he pretended to be asleep. This whole trip had gone sour, and it was her fault.

"You're in a good mood today," Lilac said.

"It's a beautiful day."

"I guess so," Lilac said.

Erin brought a plate over to the table.

"I'm really glad you're so happy," Lilac said. "I have to admit I wasn't sure how you'd react to me after last night."

"How do you mean?"

"I don't know," Lilac said. "I guess I thought you'd feel I was dirty or something. It's hard to say, exactly."

"I've never met anyone like you before, that's for sure," Erin said. "But I think you're a breath of fresh air."

"You do?"

"Sure I do. You are so free, so uninhibited. I've never known anyone like that before. Even Phil, who pretends to be all adventurous, is really pretty uptight about a lot of things."

"I'm just glad you don't hate me," Lilac said. "I'm not sure what Merry thinks about me right now."

"He did look a little green around the gills last night," Erin said.

"I think I did some real damage to our relationship."

"He'll get over it," Erin said. But Lilac wasn't so sure.

"How do you do something like that?" Erin asked. "How do you get the guts to go through with it?"

"I don't know, I guess it was kind of exciting, you know, to do this forbidden thing that just about everyone you know would disapprove of. And it gets you psyched up for it. A lot of the time it really isn't as wild as it looks. It's a lot of waiting for lighting to be set up, and you really don't have any say in who you do scenes with, and it's not so glamorous. But there are some moments, when it's just—I guess it's kind of like a high."

"I'd never have the nerve to do it," Erin said.

Lilac ate her breakfast as Erin looked on.

"I was shocked when Merry said he wanted to be in one of those movies," Erin said. "I can't picture that at all."

"I think he'll be fine," Lilac said.

"Are you swingers?"

"I beg your pardon?"

"I don't know, maybe it's too early to ask. You and Merry have only been together a short time. But, do you guys, like, do it with other couples?"

"It hasn't come up," Lilac said. "Outside of work, I guess I tend to be pretty monogamous as relationships go, anyway."

It didn't help that Lilac didn't find Phil attractive at all.

"I really don't think Merry would go for it, either." Lilac said. "So you guys are thinking about becoming swingers, huh?"

"I don't think we'd ever actually do it. But last night we were talking about it. I guess your movie got us thinking about a lot of stuff."

Lilac finished her breakfast and stood up to put her plate in the sink. Erin was staring at her.

"Do you think I'm attractive?" Erin asked.

"Yes, of course," Lilac said.

"You're very attractive," Lilac rinsed her plate and turned around. Erin was standing right beside her.

"Can you show me how to do those things?"

"What things? You're playing a joke on me, right?"

"Honestly, I'm not. I haven't done anything like that before, not even when I was younger. I mean, when I was younger I might have found another girl attractive once or twice, but I never acted on it. I never even thought about *how* I would act on it."

"What if the guys walked in on us?"

"They went to the racetrack while you were showering," Erin said. "We have all morning to ourselves. You sure you don't want to give me a crash course?"

"You've really been giving this a lot of thought," Lilac said.

"It's all I've been thinking about since that movie last night," Erin said.

"Well," Lilac said. "A good way to start is like this."

She leaned forward and pressed her lips against Erin's. The other woman's mouth opened eagerly, and they were caressing each other's tongues.

Lilac took a breath for air. "You're one eager beaver, aren't you?"

Erin wanted to kiss her more, but Lilac led her over to the table they had just eaten breakfast on. They were removing each other's clothes as they moved. Lilac cleared off the table with her free hand and pressed Erin back onto the surface with the other.

She slipped Erin's panties off, and marveled at how wet she was.

"Is this what you wanted?" Lilac said and buried her face between Erin's legs. She used her tongue, and eventually added her fingers, burying them inside her as she licked.

Erin lifted herself on her elbows, trying to see what Lilac was doing.

"Yes," Erin said between labored breaths. "Yes."

"Do you have any toys?" Lilac asked.

"In the bedroom," Erin said.

"Then let's go in there," Lilac said, stepping back and giving her room to get up.

Erin slid off the table and stood up.

"No," Lilac said. "Get on your hands and knees."

Erin obeyed and got down.

She led the way to the bedroom, and Lilac followed close behind her, occasionally slapping her on the ass.

Once in the bedroom, Erin got a dildo and a vibrator out of

the night table beside the bed on her side. Lilac took them from her and told her to get on the bed.

Then she resumed what they were doing in the kitchen, only this time Lilac incorporated the toys.

Erin's breathing turned more into grunts and inarticulate noises.

Lilac was focused on her work. She was now intent solely on making Erin come.

Hard.

CHAPTER 48

"Ari?"

"Mitch," Ariadne said hesitantly. "Is that you?"

"Ari, listen to me. I have another job for you."

"I thought something had happened to you," she said. "I never met that Reynold guy before and he said you were on another assignment. I didn't think I'd ever see you again."

"Calm down. I'm just fine. Everything is fine."

"It's just so good to hear your voice," Ariadne said. "You have no idea what was going through my head."

"I guess I do now," he said.

"There are so many things I have to talk to you about," Ariadne said.

"I know," Mitch said. "But I can't talk about all that now."

"When?" She said the words and waited, but there was no answer, only Mitch's soft breathing on the other end. He sounded so close. If she could only touch him.

"If I do this job," she said. "Will you be there?"

"Yes," Mitch said. "I promise. Will you be there?"

"When is it?"

"Tonight. At eight o'clock. A car will come for you."

"I'll be there," she said.

"Good," he said. "I knew I could count on you."

"Where *are* you, Mitch?"

He ignored her question. "I really have to go now. Things are crazy here. Go back to sleep. I'll see you tonight."

"Tonight," she said.

Then she stood there listening to the dial tone.

CHAPTER 49

"How did you do at the track?" Lilac asked.

Merry was stretched out on the bed staring at the ceiling. "Okay. I guess I broke even."

"I'm sorry about last night," she said.

Merry grunted.

"I wasn't thinking when I told Erin about the movies. And bringing a video back here, I know you must feel pretty weird. This probably hasn't been much fun for you."

"Don't worry about it," Merry said.

"You know, even if I didn't say anything, Phil would have figured it out soon enough. He's seen my movies. Guys like him are my target audience."

"I told you not to worry about it, okay? What's done is done."

When he'd returned from the horse track, Merry had found Lilac and Erin in the kitchen, talking and laughing. They really seemed to hit it off. Lilac's revelation didn't seem to hurt, if anything it seemed to have brought them closer together.

It was an interesting development, but Merry had no desire to join in. He just went right to the guest room and slid onto the bed. He was lying there when Lilac came in.

"Merry, it's too early to be in bed. Phil and Erin will wonder where we are."

"They'll just figure we're fucking," Merry said. "They probably think that's what we do twenty-four hours a day."

"What's wrong?" Lilac asked.

"Phil and I had a big fight at the track. I swear I don't know that guy anymore. I've been thinking. Maybe we should leave tomorrow."

"So soon?" Lilac asked. "But we've only been here a couple of days."

"It was a mistake to come here right now."

"Was the fight about me?"

"No, of course not," Merry said.

"Have you told Phil yet?" Lilac asked. "That we're leaving?"

"Not yet. But he probably won't be surprised."

"Can't we just stay until the end of the week? I'm really getting along great with Erin. It's been such a long time since I actually had another woman to talk to. Another woman who's not in *the business.*"

"We can stay a few more days," he said. "Just let me lie here a few minutes longer and we'll go back out there. I just need to cool down."

"Okay, I'll be out in the living room."

Lilac closed the door on her way out.

CHAPTER 50

"What're you doing?"

"Just looking at your yearbook."

Jack Underwood entered the room and stood over her. She was on the couch, flipping pages. He handed her a glass of wine. He had forgotten he had left that thing out.

"So you played football in high school, huh?" she asked. Her name was Priscilla.

"Yep. I got a football scholarship to UCLA."

"Wow," she said, looking up at him. "Were you ever pro?"

"No. I got injured the first year and sort of lost interest in everything. Too much partying, too. I flunked out. I guess I didn't take college too seriously."

"That's too bad."

"Not really. I've had a good life. Done a lot of things. I don't have too many regrets."

"Look at you," she said, looking at his photograph. "Boy, were you cute when you were young."

"How about now?"

She smiled. "Even cuter."

He laughed. "That's good to hear."

She turned the page and he saw a picture of Merry in there, over her shoulder. What a loser that guy had been. Not that he had changed much. He had been a big guy in school, but never went out for sports, always kind of kept to himself. Jack almost felt sorry for him.

Merry was the reason why he had dug out the old yearbook in the first place. Seeing that guy had made him nostalgic for old times. Jack had been at the top of the heap in high school.

Those were some of the best years he ever had.

"You done looking at that old thing?" he asked.

"Wait," she said. "Let me finish my wine first."

"Okay," he said. She was a little too interested in the yearbook. She wasn't paying attention to *him*. So he took it away from her.

"Aww, I wanted to look at it some more."

"Plenty of time for that later," he said. "I want you focused on me now."

He leaned in and kissed her.

"Okay," she said.

He took her hand and stood up. She rose to her feet as well. She had forgotten all about that stupid book.

"Let's go to the bedroom," he said. "It's a lot more comfortable in there."

"Lead the way, handsome," she said."

He bent down and swept her into his arms. She wasn't expecting it, and it clearly made an impression.

She kissed him. "This is all so romantic."

"It ain't over yet," Underwood said, carrying her across the threshold to his bedroom.

She was a stewardess. They had met in a bar. She was only in town for one night.

"You don't have much time," he said. "So I've got to make this memorable."

"It's memorable already," she told him.

He put her down on the bed. Then he started to undress her. He did it slowly, kissing her after he removed an article of clothing.

"I think I could fall in love with you, Jack Underwood."

It was probably just the wine talking, but he smiled at her.

When he had her clothes off, he looked down at her naked body. It was so beautiful. Almost perfect.

He started taking off his own clothes, standing at the foot of the bed. She watched him.

"Don't take too long," she said.

He slid into bed with her.

"Oh," she looked down at him. "You're so big."

"So I've been told."

"You're like a dream come true."

"Close your eyes."

She hesitated.

"Seriously," he said. "Close your eyes. I have a surprise for you."

She smiled and closed them.

He put his hands around her neck and squeezed. She opened her eyes wide and stared up at him, struggling beneath him, but he was strong, and it didn't take long for him to crush the life out of her.

When she stopped moving, he spread her legs apart and rammed himself inside her.

CHAPTER 51

Ariadne was waiting on the front steps when the car came. It was a long, black limousine. She stood up and grabbed her bag. *So much for being inconspicuous,* she thought.

It was running a little late. She hoped she wouldn't get blamed.

The driver got out and opened the door for her. She got inside.

All day she had been anxious about this car ride. This job. Would Mitch really be there this time? Would they have a chance to talk?

What had happened to her? She was always so calm when she had a job. So in control. But ever since that trip she took with Mitch, she was acting like an amateur. Is this what being in a relationship did to you? She had never been this way with Merry, but then again, she had never worked with Merry. This whole situation was starting to get uncomfortable.

"Would you like some music?" the driver asked after they'd been driving about five minutes.

"Okay," she said. "Something soft would be nice."

The car was dark. She looked up through the sunroof, at the moon. It was just a small crescent in the night, and looked so far away.

The driver turned on a classical station. Mozart was playing.

The drive was smooth, but took longer than she expected. As if the driver was taking the long way there.

CHAPTER 52

"I'm sorry you're not staying longer," Erin said over dinner. "We have really enjoyed having you both here. We don't get many guests."

"Well, it was really nice meeting you," Lilac said.

They were in a restaurant called The Valley, one of the nicer places near Phil and Erin's place. Phil had insisted on taking his guests out for a proper meal the night before their departure.

"Yeah, I'm sorry, too," Merry said. "But when I checked my messages and heard the one about the job interview, I figured I better get back. It's not like I get a lot of calls like that."

"So what kind of job is it, Merry?"

"For a home alarm company," he said. "I would be one of the guys responding to the calls. It actually pays a lot more than you would think."

"What about that movie you were going to do with Lilac?" Phil asked.

"I'll take things one day at a time," Merry said.

"I really hope you're not leaving early because of me," Phil said.

"Why would he leave because of you?" Erin asked.

"We haven't been getting along too well, unfortunately. We had a big argument at the track."

"What were you fighting about?"

"Nothing too serious," Merry said. "I'm just not the best company, I guess. Got a lot on my mind. This might not have been the best time to come out for a visit."

"I'm just glad you were able to come out for as long as you did," Erin said.

They were finishing up their meals, and the busboy came over to clear the table.

"Really nice meal," Merry said. "Thanks a lot, you two."

"Yeah, it was delicious," Lilac said.

"It's the least we could do," Phil said. "You coming up to see us and all."

The waiter came over and was carrying a small cake on a platter. There were lit candles in it, glowing in the dim lighting.

"You didn't."

"I just felt bad I couldn't be there for the real day," Phil said. "You know how work is."

"Happy Birthday, Merry," Erin said.

"Happy Birthday," Lilac said.

They all began to sing "Happy Birthday," as the waiter put the cake on the table and stepped back. Another waiter brought over a bottle of champagne and a metal bucket of ice.

"Happy birthday, buddy," Phil said.

Merry felt a sudden wave of emotion come over him. He had trouble articulating it.

"This is real nice."

Erin passed Merry a knife to cut the cake with, and he cut it into four pieces. The second waiter popped open the champagne and filled the glasses.

"At least we can finish your trip on a high note," Phil said.

Merry nodded and brought his glass to his lips.

"I'm really sorry we had to leave earlier than expected," he said.

But down deep, Merry was still eager to leave in the morning.

CHAPTER 53

It wasn't the same house as the one where she'd first met Reynold, but it was similar, and it looked like they were in the same neighborhood.

The driver opened her door, and she got out. "Will you be waiting for me?" she asked.

"Yes, Miss."

She went up the front steps.

The door opened before she could reach for the buzzer.

"Come in," Reynold said as he ushered her inside. "There's a chill in the air tonight, isn't there?"

"Yes," Ariadne said, and stopped in the hallway as Reynold closed and locked the door. She looked at his face as he turned to face her. He could have been handsome, but something was off. Something that made him look permanently angry.

Why do I feel so uneasy around this man? she asked herself. *I'm a fucking interrogator, for Christ's sake!*

"So nice to see you again," Reynold said. "And so soon after our last time. Please, come this way."

He started up the stairs, and she followed. A few dim lights illuminated their travels. There did not appear to be anyone else in the house with them.

They reached another hallway filled with closed doors along its length. Reynold led her to the end and stopped in front of the last door.

"I do hope you're in a particularly nasty mood tonight," he said, smiling. "You see, we have a rather stubborn subject this evening, and this may be a rather long session. We'll pay you double the usual fee, to make it worth your while. And I would appreciate you giving it your all."

"I always give it my *all*."

"Yes, of course." Reynold grabbed the knob and opened the door. They went inside.

There was a man suspended from the ceiling by thick wire that was biting into his wrists. He was standing on his tip toes, and had his back to them, but Ariadne knew who it was even before she saw the man's face.

They walked around him and stopped in front of the man. He had a ball gag in his mouth. He stared at her with pleading eyes.

"I'd introduce you," Reynold said. "But you already know Mitch, don't you?"

PART III

CHAPTER 54

"What the hell's going on here?" Ariadne asked. She was being used as a pawn in this game, and she wanted to know why.

"That's what you're here to find out," Reynold said. "And Mitch is going to provide the answers. The problem is, you might have to give him some special incentive to come clean."

Mitch continued to stare at her.

She stared back. She was not about to make any decisions about loyalties just yet. One of these men was playing her for a fool. Probably both. She found herself wondering why she had ever trusted anyone in this business. Even Mitch.

"I must say," Reynold said, with obvious admiration in his voice, "you are quite a cool customer. Last job, you did everything I asked of you, even though I know you recognized Mr. Roggert, one of Mitch's associates."

"I'm a professional," Ariadne said.

Mitch tried to speak, but the gag prevented him.

"Can I remove the gag?" Ariadne asked.

"Of course," Reynold said. "How else can he answer all our questions? No one is going to hear, by the way. The entire building is soundproofed, just for moments like this. But I have a few rules before we begin."

"Rules?" Ariadne asked. She did not make a move toward Mitch yet. "And what would they be?"

"First," Reynold said. "I must stay here in the room with you. You see, I already know most of the answers, but I want to hear them directly from Mitch. I'll be recording them, in fact, for my superiors. I'll also come in quite handy to you, my dear, since I know what the questions should be, as they may not all be evident to you. And I can let you know when he's lying, so we waste as little time as possible."

"Agreed," Ariadne said. She realized she really did not have much of a choice. Despite the illusion of this being a quiet house, she knew they weren't alone. She would be considered dangerous, and Reynold would have made sure he had back-up, just in case she decided not to cooperate.

"Secondly," Reynold continued, "you can do whatever you want to him, but you cannot release him. I am still the boss here. If I order you to cause him pain, I expect you to carry the order out."

"Agreed," she said again without hesitation, even though she still didn't know what this was about or who her allegiance was with just yet. But this was not a time for hesitation.

"Good," Reynold said, sounding genuinely pleased. "Very good."

Ariadne stood there, continuing to stare coldly at Mitch.

"You may remove the gag now."

Ariadne glanced over at Reynold, and then she leaned forward and tugged the gag down.

"Ariadne," Mitch said. "Thank God it's you!"

"*I'm* your God right now," Ariadne said. "And don't thank me just yet. I want to know what this is all about."

Reynold had been walking around the room, almost casually. Now he stood beside her, looking down at Mitch's face. Reynold was smiling. "I was wondering if I could ask a few questions, to start things off."

"I don't have anything to say to you!" Mitch snarled.

"Ariadne, I believe Mitch has forgotten that I am still his superior. Would you mind disciplining him if he crosses the boundaries of proper respect?"

Without a word, Ariadne leaned forward and struck Mitch across the face with the back of her hand. Hard. Mitch looked shocked.

Reynold smiled wider, looking like he had to keep himself from bursting out in laughter. Then he composed himself. "Remember your place, Mitch."

"If I could make a request," Ariadne said. "I would prefer if all your questions went through me."

Reynold raised an eyebrow. "Taking the initiative, are you? Very good. I was under the impression you had an aversion to asking questions."

"You're right that I don't normally do the asking, but I don't have a problem doing it. Especially in this case."

"Fine," Reynold said. "You've been very cooperative. I see no reason to deny your request."

Reynold walked away from her and around Mitch. There was a chair in the comer near the door. Reynold turned the chair around backward and sat on it, his arms resting on its back. He watched Ariadne and Mitch.

"You could begin by asking him why he's tied up like this."

Ariadne stared into Mitch's eyes. "Yes, I was wondering that myself, Mitch," she said. "Why *are* you tied up like this?"

"I have no fucking idea," Mitch said. "This is all a mistake."

She saw a glimmer of fear in Mitch's eyes. He wasn't so certain that she was on his side anymore. For some reason, that fear turned her on.

"I'm afraid this is a bad start, Ariadne," Reynold said from his chair.

"Shut up, Reynold!" Mitch said.

This time she punched him. Blood trickled from his cheek.

"You talk to me," Ariadne said. "Only me."

"Don't you want to know why he disappeared after you got back from your little vacation, Ariadne?" Reynold asked. "Or ask him how Fredericks happened to escape and make his way to your apartment."

Ariadne kept looking into Mitch's eyes. Trying to see behind the fear. Trying to see the truth. She'd been wondering about these things herself. Any doubts she'd had about Mitch seemed more justifiable now. Maybe Mitch *had* been hiding something all along. She needed to know.

Ariadne didn't ask any more questions right away. Instead, she went over to the table where she had placed her bag when they entered the room. She opened the bag and took out her tools, placing them in a silver tray on the table.

"What are you doing, Ariadne?" Mitch asked softly. "What are you going to do to me?"

"Isn't it obvious? She's going to get some answers," Reynold called out from behind Mitch.

Mitch bristled but held his tongue as he watched Ariadne pull a long golden needle from her bag, and a scalpel.

"I'll be asking you questions," Ariadne said, turning to face Mitch again. "And I want answers. The truth. You will answer the questions the first time I ask them. I will not repeat myself. Do you understand?"

Mitch swallowed hard. Something in his eyes told her that he was losing hope that he was going to get out of this alive.

"I won't repeat any of the questions."

Mitch cleared his throat. "I understand."

"Good."

CHAPTER 55

It was late when they got back to Merry's place, and they were both too tired to talk.

He sat on the couch. She kept going until she reached the bedroom. Not long afterwards, she shut off the bedroom light

Merry sat on the sofa, staring into the darkness.

Maybe Phil had been right. Maybe it was a mistake to get involved with Lilac. He would start getting possessive soon, and she would rebel against it. And the relationship would just fall apart. He could see it coming a mile away.

He should have been tired after the long drive. Lilac had no trouble going to sleep. But he had too much on his mind.

The phone rang.

"Who's calling this time of night?"

Merry got up and answered it.

"Welcome back," came the voice on the other end. "How about putting on a show for me and my friend?"

Merry didn't say anything.

"We want to see your dick in action."

Merry hung up.

He walked softly over to the bedroom and looked in. Lilac was under the covers. He had no intention of waking her up. Besides, he wouldn't be gone long.

Merry got his old Billy club out of the hall closet and retrieved the revolver he kept in a locked box on the closet's floor. He hadn't used it in a while, but he always kept it clean.

Merry went out the back way. He stayed away from streetlights and stayed close to the bushes. He didn't have any trouble jimmying the front door and getting upstairs. He did it all so quietly, no one could have heard.

When he stood in front of the man's apartment—the man who had been calling him-he hesitated.

There was light shining under the door. He wondered if this man, Finch, had any idea he was coming for him. He wondered if he should try to quietly jimmy the door or kick it in for better effect.

He softly grabbed the door knob and turned it. The door was unlocked. Merry held his breath and turned the knob all the way, pushing the door in.

"What the fuck!" the man said as Merry entered the apartment. There was a look of absolute shock on his face.

Merry had his free hand on his gun, just in case Finch had been telling the truth before, about having a gun of his own.

There was another man in the room. This new man said nothing.

Merry looked straight into the second man's eyes. And he had to fight the urge to turn his head away.

No one said anything for a few, slow-motion seconds.

Merry broke the silence with one word: "Dad?"

CHAPTER 56

"How did Fredericks escape?" Ariadne asked.

Mitch gnashed his teeth and groaned. "I let him go."

She held the long needle up to the light. "Why?"

He looked from the needle to the scalpel, resisting the urge to turn and look at Reynold, who might be coaching her from the sidelines.

"I was working for him."

"Working for him?" Ariadne asked. "But you had me interrogate him. Is that how you treat someone you work for?"

"I couldn't reveal the truth to anyone," Mitch said. "When I was told he was going to be tortured, I had to go along with it. But I made sure I was there when it happened, and I made sure it stopped before it went too far."

"I put nails through his hands. That's not too far?"

"You didn't kill him."

"So when you got him alone, you set him free?"

"Yes."

"Ask him how he accomplished that," Reynold said from the shadows.

"Yes, how did you accomplish it?"

Mitch didn't respond. She grabbed the needle and plunged it deep into his kneecap without a moment's hesitation. He shouted from the pain.

"Well?"

Mitch stared up into her eyes. A tear rolled down one of his cheeks.

"I made it look like some people from the outside got in and sprang him. But I had to create the illusion that I was trying to recapture him."

"And you *did* recapture him."

"Yes I did, because he went to see you."

"And why did he come to see me?"

Mitch hesitated again. She brought the scalpel close to his face.

"He knew about you," Mitch said. "He'd had you investigated. Partly because he knew I had feelings for you. But you also have quite the reputation. Fredericks thought you would be a good ally for our cause. He had the man driving his getaway car stop at your apartment building. He was probably delirious at that point. I can't imagine he was thinking clearly. I didn't want him to approach you because I knew you wouldn't trust him, and because there was a chance he would blow my cover to you."

"So you had to try to stop him from reaching me?"

"Yes, I had to actually recapture him because he wouldn't listen to me"

"And you had no clue he was going to do this?"

"The driver called me after Fredericks went inside your building. He was confused. It was not part of the plan."

"This Fredericks sounds insane," Ariadne said. "Trying to approach a woman who had just tortured him, when he could have gotten away."

"He was a fanatic," Mitch said. "He thought that perhaps, in a different setting, he could talk to you. Convince you."

"Convince me of *what*? His cause?"

"Not everything the 'powers that be' do is moral or right."

"Sounds like treason to me," Reynold said from his perch.

Ariadne shot him a look. Then she looked back down at Mitch. "So what was Mr. Fredericks' cause?"

"He's a religious man," Mitch said. "Someone like Reynold would call him a fanatic."

"More like a terrorist," Reynold said.

"And you shared his cause?"

Mitch did not respond.

Ariadne turned to Reynold, who nodded. She stepped forward and cut off the tip of Mitch's nose. The chunk of flesh fell to the floor, and blood dripped down his face, covering his lips.

"Goddammit," Mitch said. "I felt his cause was just. I also shared his *money*. The guy was a billionaire. And I've been unhappy with my work the last couple of years."

"Unhappy enough to take up with terrorists," Reynold said. "How noble."

Mitch stared down at the large needle sticking out of his knee. He gritted his teeth again.

"Why did you take me on vacation?" she asked

"After the Fredericks thing, I wanted to get out of town and give things a chance to cool off."

"They didn't connect you to the escape?"

"I didn't think so," he said. "Not then. I had planned it all down to the last detail."

"Why *me*?"

Mitch looked up at her. His face told her he didn't understand the question.

"Why take me with you when you left?"

"Because I wanted you with me."

"So you really did want a relationship with me?"

"Yes, Ariadne. Is that so hard to believe?"

"Bullshit," Reynold said from behind her.

She leaned forward and slowly cut around Mitch's eyes, removing the flesh of his eyelids. There was more blood, mixing with tears now. She took a second needle and held it in front of one of his eyes. He could not blink.

"Is that the truth? Or was it that you thought I was lonely and vulnerable, and that maybe you could get me to fall in love with you, and you could convert me to your cause? Or maybe you could use me as a scapegoat?"

Mitch stared past her, at the wall.

"Did you fall in love with me, Mitch?"

"Yes," he said softly.

"Bullshit," Reynold said again. "Can't you see he's playing you for a fool?"

"Yes, I did, Ariadne. I *do* love you."

She plunged the needle into his left eye. He jerked and

grunted in the chair, struggling at his bonds. Then he could hold it in no longer, and let out a scream.

"We've learned a lot here today," she said, when he had quieted down. "That you're a traitor. That you're a user. That you would have used me for your own ends if you could have seduced me into trusting you."

"No, Ariadne," Mitch said. "If I was going to betray you, I would have. But I didn't. You know that."

"Not then, but who knew what your plan was when you got back. You must have thought I was pretty stupid," she said. "Just another stupid girl you could manipulate just by telling me you loved me."

"Ariadne," he said. "You know that's not true. I never thought you were stupid. That I could fool you. I wouldn't have even tried to do that. I took you with me in an act of desperation. I didn't know how much longer I would be safe, and I wanted to spend some time with you before it all came to an end."

"Make him tell you everything he said about you when we questioned him the first time," Reynold said. "Make him admit how he used you."

Mitch looked up at her with his one good eye. "Ariadne."

"If you say my name again, I'll kill you."

"Kill me? Ariadne, please."

She sliced off the rest of his nose. Blood spattered his clothes.

"Go ahead," Reynold said. "Finish him off. We've got more than enough evidence against him at this point. I just wanted you to hear it for yourself."

The fact Reynold had no visible recording device made her realize there had to be a hidden camera somewhere in the room. Someone else was watching and recording their session.

She held his right eye wide open with her fingers, and sliced it with the scalpel, like she had seen once in a movie by Luis Bunuel and Salvador Dali. She remembered its name. *Un Chien Anadalou*. It was so much messier in real life.

He screamed loudly again, as blood and optical fluid ran down his cheek. His face was thick with blood by this time, and it was all over his clothes. The chair he was tied to clattered loudly against the floor as he struggled to pull free.

She turned and looked at Reynold. He was smiling enthusiastically. He shot out his hand, and turned his thumb down like some Roman emperor.

She leaned forward and ran the scalpel across Mitch's throat. It didn't take much pressure, and it cut so deeply that, if she had pressed a little harder, she could have severed his head. Instead, she cut just deep enough to sever his jugular.

With his death, the session ended.

CHAPTER 57

"What the hell are you talking about?"

Merry stared at the man he knew was his father. He was older, and Merry had only seen him in person once before, but he still recognized the man. He was determined to finally get some answers.

The man stood there, petrified. Merry had no idea what was going through his head, but he suspected the man recognized him, too. From the beating all those years ago. It wasn't like he had hidden his face.

Finch, the peeping tom and obscene phone caller who had set all this in motion, now had something new to watch, but he had grown indignant at having it unfold in his apartment.

"Harvey, what is this all about?" Peeping Tom said. "Are you really this maniac's father?"

Harvey said nothing. Merry remembered the Billy club in his hand and had a fleeting thought. Maybe he should *beat* the truth out of him.

But Harvey's face told him he was confused. Scared.

"Please," Harvey said. "Don't hurt me."

"What the fuck are you going to do with that thing?" Finch shouted. "What the fuck are you doing in my apartment! I'm going to call the cops."

"Make one move toward that phone, pervert," Merry said, "and I'll cave your skull in."

"He means it, Jay," Harvey said.

"You know this guy?" Jay asked. "Is he really your son?"

"No," Harvey said. "I don't have any children."

"No?" Merry asked. "You really don't remember Mary

Campbell? The woman you knocked up and left to fend for herself?"

"Mary Campbell?" Harvey asked.

"Ha!" Jay said. "You got the wrong man, buddy! Harvey here is as queer as a three-dollar bill."

"Of course, I remember Mary," Harvey said. His mouth must have been dry, because he licked his lips nervously. "But I didn't get her pregnant."

"You sure about that?" Merry asked.

"I don't know anything about a child," Harvey said.

"Can you be 100 percent sure she wasn't pregnant when you left?" Merry asked. "That you aren't my father?"

"Your mother was probably a whore," Jay said. "How can you be sure *who* your father was?"

Merry hit the man in the shoulder with the Billy club, knocking him against a wall. Jay cried out and lunged at him, and Merry hit him again, knocking him to the floor. "You stay out of this, you sick fuck," Merry said. "I'll settle my score with you later."

"I'll kill you," Jay said, gritting his teeth. He was holding his arm.

"Try it," Merry said. "Do me that favor. So I can cripple you for life."

"Shut up, Jay," Harvey said. "Can't you see this man is dangerous?"

"You know that from experience, don't you, old man?"

"I know you," Harvey said. "I remember that day in the parking lot. You were a kid. You and that friend of yours."

Merry was amazed at his own calmness. "I think about that day all the time, too. I've always been ashamed of what I did."

"Ashamed?" Harvey asked.

"Yes," Merry said. "Ashamed."

They looked at each other in silence. Merry could hear Jay in the corner, moving.

"Stay where you are, asshole!" Merry said without turning to look at the man.

"Do what he says," Harvey said.

"This is my place," Jay said, on his knees now. "I don't want him here. Take this somewhere else."

"It's because of you I'm here," Merry said. "You and your sick phone calls and you watching me. Did you know about your friend's hobbies, Dad? He's a freak who likes to spy on people and taunt them about it. A disgusting freak."

"Don't call me that, you crazy bastard" Jay said.

"Look, I'm not your father," Harvey said. "Honest, I'm not."

"You're telling me you never slept with her?"

"Look, I was mixed-up back then. I'm certainly not the first person who ever tried to change what I was, to try to live what I thought was a *normal* life. Sure, I cared about Mary, but it was doomed from the start. We both knew that. She wanted so badly for me to be something I wasn't. But I couldn't have gotten her pregnant. She never said a word about that. She didn't say anything when I left."

"You left so quickly—how can you be sure?"

"She could have found me again if she wanted to," Harvey said. "Back then I was trying to find some answers about myself. I was young. I was confused. I thought I was attracted to her, that I could go straight. We tried to make it work, but it was a lie. I left, sure. But I wouldn't abandon her with a baby."

"How do you know that?"

"She would have told me, wouldn't she?"

"Maybe she didn't want to force you to keep living a lie. Who knows what was going through her head," Merry said.

Harvey licked his dry lips again. "Can I sit down?"

"I want you two out of here," Jay said from the floor. "I want you the fuck out of my place."

"You're really tempting me to hurt you again, asshole," Merry said.

"Shut up, Jay," Harvey said. "Don't make things worse."

"Worse? This fucker probably broke my arm."

"That'll just be the beginning if you don't shut the fuck up," Merry said, glaring at the man.

"If you thought I was your father, why did you attack me that day?"

Merry turned his attention back to Harvey. "I was a kid. I

was angry. You had abandoned me and my mother. I wanted to settle the score."

"Who told you I was your father?" Harvey asked. "Was it Mary? Did she tell you that?"

"She had a picture of you. But no, she would never talk about it. She wanted to keep it a secret from me, too. Maybe she had some shame of her own about it. I'll never know for sure. You see, she isn't alive anymore."

"I'm sorry," he said. "So who told you?"

"My grandmother. She saw the picture and told me who you were. I didn't know if I could believe her at the time, but it was the only time someone ever gave me answers about where I came from. Who my father was."

"How do you know she wasn't lying?"

"Because I asked my mother, and she looked so miserable when I confronted her about it. She wouldn't say a word, but her eyes, they said it all. And that time in the parking lot, when I saw you in the flesh, and you looked just like you did in that picture, all I could think of was my mother's eyes. That's what set me off."

"What happened to your mother?" Harvey asked. "You said she'd died."

"Cancer," Merry said. "She died a couple of years ago. But she raised me. She did the best she could."

"I wish I could tell her I'm sorry." Harvey said.

"For as long as I can remember, she was never a very happy woman, and you couldn't have been the only tragic thing in her life."

"So, no more violence?"

"Not unless you give me a reason for it."

"I still find it hard to believe I could be your father," Harvey said again. "After all this time. She never contacted me. She could have tracked me down somehow. I would have helped her raise you."

"You didn't want to be with her, and she knew it," Merry said. "And she might not have been happy, but she did have pride. And she wasn't the type to beg for anything."

"Look, if I hurt her, I'm sorry. Really I am. We were both young and foolish."

"Maybe at one time I thought I could judge you. But I've had a lot of time to think about what I did to you in that parking lot. And I don't think I have the right to judge you anymore."

"So what happens now?"

"Nothing," Merry said. "You may be my biological father, but you were never a real father to me, and we can't change that now. I'm only grateful to have this chance to say I'm sorry for what I did to you."

"You really regret that?"

"Yes, I do. Does that surprise you?"

"I don't know," he said.

"She was always working when I was a kid. I pretty much raised myself. I've always made my own choices. Good or bad. I'm not about to blame you or her for my life. I'm not one of those people who weep about the past. I've moved on."

"Wonderful!" Jay cried out from the comer. "I'm so glad for you!"

"Your friend here is treading on thin ice," Merry said. "He's been looking at me though windows and calling me on the phone, asking me about my dick. You tell your friend if he continues to do these things, I'm going to slice *his* dick off and feed it to him. And the only reason I'm not doing it tonight is because you're here, and it gave me a chance to right an old wrong."

"I'll talk some sense into him," Harvey said.

"Like hell you will," Jay said.

"If he doesn't shut up, I'm going to knock out his teeth," Merry said.

Harvey shot his friend a look. Jay didn't say anything.

"I can't say I think much of your choice in friends," Merry said.

"Do you mind if I ask you your name?" Harvey asked.

Merry winced and then said, "Merry."

"Sounds like your mother's name," Jay said mockingly.

"Merry," Merry said, "like Merry fucking Christmas. Merry, as in happy. I remember lots of times her crying over nothing. I guess my name proved she had a sense of humor about it all. I always hated it. Over the years, I thought a lot about changing it, but I never did. I guess I've gotten used to it."

"I like it," Harvey said. But Merry thought he was just saying it because he didn't know what else to say.

"I'm going to leave now," Merry said. "I've said all I have to say."

"Is there anything I can do?" Harvey said. "I mean, I don't know what I could do, but if everything you said is true, I feel like I owe you something."

"You don't owe me anything." He turned and glared at Jay, who was still on his knees, afraid or unable to stand up. "You forget you ever saw me," Merry said to him. "You stop watching me. You stop calling me. You get a real life. Or you'll be sorry you didn't."

Jay still held his shoulder, glaring at Merry with pure hatred.

"He won't bother you anymore."

Merry went to the door, opened it.

He looked back one last time, and then he left.

He felt the gun under his belt and was glad he hadn't needed to use it.

CHAPTER 58

"It was him!" Merry said.

"Who?" Lilac asked, sitting up in bed.

"My father."

"Where? What are you talking about?"

"I saw him."

"Where were you?"

"I got another one of those calls," Merry said. "And I went over there to bust that pervert's head open, and he was there."

"Your father is the guy who's been calling you?" Lilac asked. "The peeping tom?"

"No," Merry said. "But he was there, in the guy's apartment. They knew each other. They must be friends. Or lovers."

"So is your father some nut, too?"

"No," Merry said. "Oh, I don't know. He didn't seem to be."

"Then what was he doing there? Are you certain it was him?"

"It was him," Merry said. "I never thought I'd see him again, but there he was. It was so strange, I didn't believe it was real at first. What are the chances I'd go over to that asshole's place and find my father standing there? It doesn't make sense to me. But I do know that after all these years, I was able to say I was sorry for that time when I was a kid and I attacked him. And I was able to tell him about my mother."

"What did he say?"

"He listened," Merry said. "He seemed to have a reaction to what I had to say. He actually seemed human after all."

"Well, you knew he was human."

"You know what I mean," Merry said. "He seemed to have a

heart. To regret what he did. He honestly had no idea my mother was pregnant when he left her."

"So what happens now?" Lilac asked.

"I don't know if I'll ever see him again," Merry said. "It was so much of its moment. It just felt good to finally say all the things I wanted to say to him for so long."

"If it went well, why didn't you invite him back here?"

"I didn't even think about it. And I don't think he'd want to anyway. I mean, it was a lot to unload on him. I think he's still in shock. When I got there, I was ready to break some bones, and when I left, it was like this catharsis. Like this burden was lifted from me, you know? I almost forgot why I had gone over there in the first place."

"Don't you want to ever see him again, talk some more?"

"I want to get out of here," Merry said.

"Huh?"

"Ask Tony to send us the tickets now. I want to go to Florida a little early. I want to get away from here for a while. I just want a change. This place has been depressing me so much. And I want to start fresh with you."

"Me, too," Lilac said.

There was the buzz of the doorbell. Merry went over to the intercom and pushed the button.

"Yeah, who's there?"

"Merry?" a man's voice said. "Can I come up? This is Harvey. Jay told me where you lived"

Merry stood there for a few minutes.

"Merry? Are you there?"

"Is it your father?" Lilac asked.

"Yeah," Merry said. "He wants to come up."

"So let him up."

"It's kind of late, isn't it?"

"What are you talking about? You were just over there, weren't you? Let him come up, for Christ's sake!"

"Merry?" said the voice from the intercom.

"Come on up," Merry said, pressing the buzzer to let him in. "I'm on the third floor."

CHAPTER 59

When she got downstairs, Reynold was waiting for her. He was not alone.

There were three other men, all wearing business suits.

She'd been able to take a shower and change her clothes.

She couldn't leave covered in blood, and if they had wanted her dead, they would have killed her already.

Ariadne looked at Reynold. "Can I go now?"

"Of course you can," Reynold said. "You did real good tonight. I'll see you get that bonus."

She looked around at the other men. At least one of them was another interrogator.

"I'll call you when we have another job for you," Reynold said.

She was going to tell him it was over, that she quit. But it didn't seem like the right time. She just wanted to get out of there.

"Just one question before I go," Ariadne said, playing it cool.

"Sure," Reynold said. "Anything."

"You were sure about all the things he'd done," Ariadne said. "How did you know I didn't have anything to do with it all? I mean, I did go away with him. Doesn't that make me look bad?"

She was able to ask, because she was sure she had proven her loyalty. She almost wished she hadn't. But it was important to gauge his reaction. She wanted to know if she'd be next on the chopping block.

"We have eyes everywhere," Reynold said, and laughed. "We're like fucking Santa Claus. We know who's been naughty and who's been nice. And we make sure the bad ones suffer. But you, you're good. Real good. And we take care of our own."

"I'm glad to hear it."

"Don't go losing any sleep about it," Reynold said. "We know we can trust you."

"Have a pleasant evening," Reynold said. "The car's out front. And don't worry, I won't be calling you too soon. Take a week off. Enjoy yourself. You've earned it."

"Thanks," Ariadne said.

"Man, the way you iced Mitch," one of the other men said. "Merciless!"

They all laughed.

Ariadne smiled as Reynold opened the front door.

She walked down the steps and didn't look back. The driver was already holding the car door open for her.

"Going home?" the driver asked.

"Sure," Ariadne said, sliding inside.

What the hell did I just do? she thought, desperately holding back tears.

CHAPTER 60

"I'm sorry to disturb you," Harvey said. "I just had to see you again before I left."

"You want anything at all? A beer?"

"I'll get it," Lilac said. "You want one too, Merry?"

"Sure," he said, watching her head toward the kitchen.

"This all took me by surprise. I mean, to go through life thinking you never had a child, and then to see a man who claims to be your son—and it's a plausible story, the more I think about it. It really shook me up."

Lilac came back and handed opened bottles to Harvey and Merry. They both took swigs.

"It was a shock to me too," Merry said.

"I don't know what it was," Harvey said. "But when you attacked me as a kid. There was something about your face. I knew it wasn't just a random attack. That there was a reason for it, or you seemed to think there was. That's why I never pursued it with the police. I told them that I didn't get a good look at you guys, and there weren't any other reliable witnesses. Maybe it was the way you looked at me that made me keep it secret, maybe it was my own self-loathing at the time. I had a lot of it back then. And in some sick way I might have felt I deserved what I got."

"But you didn't," Merry said. "It was the worst thing I ever did in my life. I always regretted it. Always wished I could have erased it."

"I can't stay," Harvey said. "I have to get a flight in a couple of hours. I live in Phoenix now. I was in the area on business and thought I'd check in on Jay. I haven't seen him in a while.

But I didn't expect any of this."

"Do you need a ride to the airport?"

"I have a rental car," Harvey said. "I'm all set."

Merry took a long pull from his beer.

"Don't judge Jay too harshly," Harvey said. "He gets drunk and does stupid things. I think I convinced him to stop bothering you."

"It's been going on for a while now. And he was really starting to piss me off."

"That's some strange friend you have," Lilac said.

"He has his own problems," Harvey said. "Sometimes he has a sick sense of humor."

"I guess," Merry said, still ticked off when he thought of those phone calls.

Harvey put down the beer. He had taken a few sips. "I really have to get going. I don't know why I came here. I guess I just wanted to see you in a less hostile environment."

"Well, it's been an interesting night."

"And then some," Harvey said. "Listen, if you really are my son, I just wanted to ask you…. ask you to forgive me. I had no idea."

"Sure, I can forgive you," Merry said. "If you can forgive me for what I did to you."

"I can."

"Then so can *I*."

Harvey stood up and straightened his clothes, self-consciously. "I feel like we accomplished something tonight."

Merry walked him to the door.

"It was nice to meet you," Harvey said, turning toward Lilac on the way out.

"Same here."

"Here's my card," Harvey said, handing it to Merry. "I've written my home number on the back. Call me if you ever get the urge, okay? I mean, I don't expect us to have any kind of normal relationship after all that's happened, but if you ever want to talk some more, feel free to call."

"Okay," He didn't make any effort to write down his number for Harvey. "Thanks."

"And if you don't call, I understand that too," Harvey said. "Well, I guess this is it. Nice to have met you both."

"It was good to meet you," Merry said. "To tie up loose ends."

Harvey went out into the hallway, and Merry watched him head down the stairs. He went back inside and locked the door.

"That was different, huh?" Lilac asked.

"You said it. It's late. Let's get some sleep, okay?"

"Okay," Lilac said, and headed back toward the bedroom.

Merry finished his beer and went into the kitchen to toss the bottle. Then he looked at his father's business card. He worked for some agency, though it wasn't clear what kind of company it was. He flipped it over and looked at the phone number written in blue ink. He tore the card to shreds and dropped the pieces into the garbage. Then he shut off the lights and went to bed.

CHAPTER 61

When Ariadne got back to her apartment, she locked all the doors and rushed to the bathroom, where she threw up everything in her stomach.

When she was done, she stayed on her knees, hugging the toilet bowl, trying to force herself to throw up more. But that was it.

She kept picturing Mitch's face as she took his life away, and it horrified her. All the years of brutality by her hands. What was it that man had said? That she was *merciless*. And he'd said it with *glee*.

Yes, she was merciless. But killing Mitch had done something to her. Despite the fact that he had been a fool and had probably tried to use her, she had not wanted to kill him. But she didn't dare show any hesitation in front of Reynold, or remorse. Now that she was alone, she could let her guard down. That look on Mitch's face before she slit his throat, that pleading look in his eyes that told her to just end it. Now, with no one else around, she could feel the pain.

She thought of Reynold and his cohorts. She found herself repulsed by all the people she had to interact with in her job. People she no longer wanted to deal with.

She closed her eyes and tried to empty her mind, but it wouldn't work. Pictures kept playing over and over again of Mitch and those pleading eyes. Of the way those same eyes rolled up into his head when she cut his throat. .

Ariadne tried to vomit one last time. Nothing came up.

She got to her feet and looked in the mirror.

Her face was tired. Worn. The face of a woman defeated.

I have to end this, she thought. *It might be time for me to change professions.*

After all this time, she had finally lost her stomach for it.

Had she killed the wrong man today? She didn't dare sleep. She didn't want to see Mitch in her dreams that night.

CHAPTER 62

"Those were the good old days," Jack Underwood said as he flipped through the pages of his high school yearbook. "It seems so long ago, like a past life or something, you know?"

His guest couldn't answer.

"It's strange how fast life goes by" he said, turning to face her on the bed. "But I don't have to tell you that."

He was flipping through the pages of the yearbook. All the girls he'd fucked back then. He had been able to perform well enough—he never had a problem with that—but he never felt truly satisfied. It wasn't until he'd iced a few that he really got turned on. But high school was still an innocent time. He hadn't made his first kill yet, well, his first *human* kill, and he had been pretty popular without really trying. Hell, he hadn't tried *at all*.

He looked at the team photos. He'd been a good player. Pictures of his buddies filled him with regret—he hadn't really stayed in touch with any of them. Once he went out west, he kind of left this life behind. He half-heartedly thought about looking one up now that he was living here again, giving him a call.

But it wouldn't work. They were probably all married now, with the accompanying burdens and responsibilities to soften them up. Maybe some were in jail. No matter what happened to them, he wouldn't have much in common with them anymore.

He came across a photo of Merry. It was funny, how he had never really looked at it before. Never any reason to. In high school, Merry had been a nothing. He had only acknowledged Merry's existence to cut him down, humiliate him. Even that didn't have much appeal. Underwood thought about Merry now. He was still a loser. Couldn't even keep a job as a cop. It was a hell of a lot more manly a job than Underwood ever would have expected from such a geek, but people changed.

What did Lilac see in a guy like that, anyway?

It was so strange seeing Merry again. It brought up a flood of emotions he hadn't felt in years. Emotions that felt kind of alien now. Looking at the yearbook brought on the same kind of feelings. Stuff he couldn't explain.

He tried to remember what it was a like to be a kid. To have it easy. To not have a care in the world. It seemed so far away. Too much had happened since then.

"You want to do it again," he said to his stewardess. "I'm game if you are."

She just kept staring at the ceiling with those glassy eyes.

CHAPTER 63

Merry woke with a shout. He was having one of his dreams again. This time he couldn't remember it at all, but he woke terrified, soaked in sweat.

"Merry?" Lilac was saying. "Are you okay?"

He looked around. He was sitting in an airplane seat. Some of the other people nearby were craning their necks to look at him.

"Are you all right, sir?" a stewardess asked.

"I'm fine," Merry said. "Just a bad dream."

"Is there anything I can do?" the stewardess asked.

"No," Merry said. "I'll be fine."

"Man, that must have been some dream," Lilac said.

"I was running from someone. I can't remember who it was," he said. "But yeah, it must have been bad. Are we almost there?"

"About another hour or so," Lilac said. She had her arm snaked through his.

"I guess I just don't like flying," Merry said.

"Really?" Lilac asked. "I kind of like it. Always have. I feel like a kid again, on an amusement park ride or something, you know?"

"I guess so."

"If you hate flying so much, it's a wonder you got to sleep so easily."

"I took a tranquilizer before the flight. Too bad it wasn't stronger."

She looked out her window, down at the world below. "It's so beautiful from up here."

He didn't turn to look. He couldn't take it just yet.

Merry just closed his eyes. He couldn't get back to sleep, but it made the trip a little easier to bear.

CHAPTER 64

"I've been thinking about it, Francie, and I think I'm going to quit."

"Can you do that?" Francie said. "I mean, is it that easy?"

"I don't know. I doubt it. But I don't care anymore. I don't enjoy it anymore. My heart just isn't in it."

"So what were you planning to do today?"

"I don't know," Ariadne said. "Don't you have to be at your job?"

"Not today," Francie said. "I have the day off. In fact, it's kind of funny you're talking about quitting and all, because I quit my job. I just couldn't stand being in that office anymore. I was climbing the walls."

"Are you serious? What are you going to do now?"

"I have some money saved. I think I'll take my time figuring it out. I haven't taken any time off in a long time, and I want to savor it."

"If you can afford to do it, that's great."

"Do you know when your next job is?" Francie asked. "I mean, I know you're thinking about quitting and all, but I guess what I want to know is if you're going to be free for a while."

"I guess so," Ariadne said, but, in truth, she had no idea what she was going to do next.

"Have you heard from Mitch at all?"

Ariadne glared at her without even realizing it. The name triggered so many associations Ariadne did not want to be reminded of so early in the morning. It almost seemed as if Francie had said it on purpose, as if she knew he was dead. But, how could she? Ariadne chocked it up to paranoia, a hazard of her occupation. It was probably just jealousy she'd detected in Francie's voice.

"Did I hit a nerve?" Francie asked, trying to sound innocent.

"Things between me and Mitch are over," Ariadne said, still not sure how she felt about it.

"For good?"

"Forever."

"I'm sorry to hear that," Francie said. "Was it a messy breakup?"

"You could say that."

"No wonder you look so awful this morning."

"Thanks a lot."

"Do you want to talk about it?"

"No."

"I think we should really do something special today, to get your mind off it."

"I don't know if I feel up to it."

"Come on. You just said before you could use the company. We're both free, right? Let's act free."

"What do you have in mind?"

"I don't know," Francie said, and thought about it. "A little shopping. A nice lunch. Maybe go for drinks a little later."

"What the hell. I can't just sit around here all day. Let me get dressed."

CHAPTER 65

Tony met them at the airport.

"So how was the trip?" he asked.

"Fine," Merry said. He put the suitcases down for a minute, while Lilac kissed Tony's cheek.

"So where are we staying?" she asked.

"I was going to put you up in a hotel," Tony said. "But like I told you, we somehow got ahold of this mansion. A buddy of mine is the caretaker while the owners are away traveling around the world or some shit. It's the most fucking incredible place you've ever seen. I don't even know how many rooms. So you might as well stay there. It's bigger than most hotels I've seen."

"Sounds wild," Lilac said.

"You want me to take one of those?" Tony asked Merry.

"No thanks," Merry said. "I can handle it."

"Okay, follow me." Tony led the way.

They followed him out of the baggage claim area and through the doors that led to the parking lot.

"So I have this place for a month if I need it," Tony said. "But I only plan to stick around for two weeks. Since you guys got here so early, we're going to start filming tomorrow. I've got some other guys helping me. I'm going to film four or five movies at once; there are so many fucking rooms there won't be any overlap. I even invited a couple of director buddies out to take advantage of it."

They reached Tony's car. It was a new model, very flashy. Tony popped the trunk.

"We're filming tomorrow?" Merry asked, putting the suitcases in.

"Don't worry, Merry," Lilac said. "It will be fun."

"Yeah, and you'll get your money all the sooner too," Tony said.

"Who else is there?" Lilac asked.

"I called everyone I could get hold of," Tony said. "It'll be like old home week."

"Is Underwood going to be there?" Merry asked.

Tony grimaced. "He might come later, but you guys will be long gone by then. You got a problem with him, huh?"

"I don't know," Merry said. "We're not exactly pals, that's all."

"Don't worry about it," Tony said. "Like I said, you two will start filming tomorrow. You'll be gone by the end of the week."

"And if you want to do some girl-girl scenes, too, that'd be great." Tony said to Lilac.

Lilac looked at Merry. "I'm up for it."

"But I guess you don't want to do any other guys, huh?"

"I'd rather not."

"You might want to rethink that for future work," Tony said. "But that should be okay this time around. I have more than enough people to fill in."

"Great."

They all got in and Tony started the engine. "Listen to that purr. I just got this car three days ago. Just off the line. Ain't she a beaut?"

"Sure is," Merry said.

"Who knows," Tony said. "If you're pretty good at this, you might be able to afford a car like this someday too."

CHAPTER 66

"So what do you think?" Francie asked.

They had been drinking for a while, and Ariadne was refilling their glasses with vodka and orange juice.

"I don't know," Ariadne said, deliberately stalling.

"What don't you know?" Francie demanded.

"I kind of like my independence."

"So do I. But you can't tell me you don't get lonely. Just this morning you were telling me you wanted some company."

"Yeah, sure. I get like that sometimes. But not all the time. Sometimes I like to be alone."

"This place is big enough. If you want to be alone, we can get out of each other's way. Come on, Ari, let me move in."

"I don't know."

"I'm over here so much, it's like I live here already."

"That's true enough."

"Come on, give me a chance."

"What about sleeping arrangements."

"You've got that spare room. I could sleep there if you want."

"My office?"

"I wouldn't want to put you out. Then again, you do have a nice, big bed."

"I knew it!"

"Look, you can't tell me you're not curious about it."

"About what?" Ariadne said. "Sex with you?"

Francie laughed.

"Now I really don't know."

"Bullshit," Francie said. "I see right through you, you know. I really do. You pretend to be so uptight about it, but down deep you really want to try it. I can't believe you've held out for so long. I know you want to find out what it's like. And, baby, I would love to show you. And I'd show you right, I'd do you like nobody has ever done you."

"How do you know I'd ever go that way?"

"Stop being coy, will you? How many times have we shared a playful kiss? There were a couple of times I thought it would go beyond that, but you always held back, and I never forced you."

"You couldn't force me if you wanted to!"

"But I saw that part of you, and I know it exists. You told me yourself it was over between Mitch and you."

"That doesn't mean I want to change my sexual preference, for Christ's sake," Ariadne said, and then her eyes misted over. "Look, don't mention him anymore, okay?"

"Okay," Francie said, retreating for a moment, probably afraid she'd stepped over the line.

"Look, maybe I do get curious sometimes," Ariadne said.

As she said the words, she found herself thinking that she really did want some human contact right now. She wanted to be held and loved, and she was much too tired to go carousing. And Francie was damned cute. Ariadne had known for the longest time that Francie wanted her, and she'd denied her for so long that it was starting to get ridiculous.

"And?" Francie asked, unable to read Ariadne's reaction. Either she was going to admit she was interested, or she was going to start crying.

"And I've been resisting it," Ariadne said, "because I just didn't think I was up for it. And I guess I've always been afraid that, if things didn't work out, we could ruin our friendship."

"I'd treat you real good," Francie said. "And if at any point you want to stop it, that's fine. No hard feelings."

Ariadne drained her glass and refilled it with vodka.

"I really wish you'd give me a chance. You really turn me on, Ariadne. You always have, and I'd love to make you happy."

Ariadne thought about it.

"Well, as far as moving in together goes, let's put that on the back burner. But as for making love. What the hell. Let's do it."

"You're serious?" Francie said, amazed.

"Sure I am! It might be the liquor talking, but I want to see what it's all about."

"Okay."

Francie put her drink down and grabbed Ariadne's hand.

"Come on," Francie said. "I want to get started before you change your mind!"

CHAPTER 67

Merry got out of the shower and wrapped himself in a big, fluffy towel. Everything was so big in this house. He felt dwarfed by it all. Lilac was in front of the mirror applying her makeup. He watched her as he dried himself off.

"You still nervous?"

"I guess so."

"Don't be," she told him. "It's no big deal. Just try to forget the camera's there."

"Easy for you to say," he said. "You're a pro."

"That's right," she said. "So listen to me."

The bathroom was huge. It didn't have a bathtub submerged in the floor like some of the other bathrooms, but it had a big, roomy shower stall, and there was a lot of space between the shower and the sink and the toilet. Room to walk around.

He'd never even seen hotel rooms this nice. The bedroom was even bigger. A giant, king-size bed. All kinds of cabinets and a big, deep closet. Thick carpeting that felt silky beneath his bare feet. It was almost like being royalty.

"How soon do we have to be downstairs?"

"In about an hour or so," she said. "We have time for breakfast."

"I'm not hungry. Not at all."

"Butterflies, huh?"

"Fucking bats," he said.

"You've really got to relax. There's absolutely nothing for you to be nervous about. I'll be right there with you! Maybe you could use a drink before the shoot."

"I don't know."

"We'll see," she said. "You'll be fine."

"How many scenes are you doing today?"

"Two or three. Then I have a couple tomorrow. Then we'll leave."

"Pretty short stay, huh?"

"The money's really good for a short stay, though."

"I know. I could really use it."

He turned on the blow dryer they'd brought along and dried his hair. The mirror was big and he could even see her behind him. She was trimming her pubic hair a little. They hadn't had sex in a couple of days and he was pretty hot for her. It should help when they started shooting.

He tried not to think about what would happen if he couldn't get it up or something like that. If the cameras intimidated him too much. He definitely had no intention of talking about it, and he tried not to *think* about it, but it was there in the back of his mind. He couldn't fool himself. Not completely.

He started getting dressed, and Lilac smiled at him. He could see her in the mirror, behind him. He turned to look at her.

"Everything's going to be fine," she told him. "You'll see."

"I know," he said, watching her wash off what was left of the shaving cream. He already had a hard-on.

CHAPTER 68

Underwood was thinking about the first time he'd ever fucked a dead woman. How hot he had gotten. How it had almost driven him nuts with lust. Sometimes he thought about it during a shoot and got really excited. It worked every time.

He thought about it now, for some reason, in the airport terminal. He was waiting for his bags. Reggie, this tall, lean black guy who also did porn was there to pick him up. He was probably the closest thing Underwood had to a friend in the industry. He wasn't really close to too many people.

He thought most of the people he met in the business were freaks, losers. Most of the women were kind of pathetic. He liked the life—it was easy money—and it was kind of funny, knowing he was a porn star. And he was good at it. He'd stumbled into the whole thing and it had lasted. It was lucrative. But he didn't have much respect for the other people involved.

Then again, he really didn't have much respect for *anyone*.

"How was the flight, man?" Reggie asked. He was watching the suitcases go 'round and 'round on the conveyor belt.

"It was okay," Underwood said. "I wasn't due in until the end of the week, but I was kind of bored and thought I'd come out early."

"That's cool," Reggie said. "Gives me someone I can talk to."

"I thought everyone was here," Underwood said. "Tony said it was like a fucking convention or something."

"Yeah. But I don't know. I don't relate to the some of the younger guys. They're a bunch of cowboys. Big dicks and no fucking brains, you know?"

"I hear ya," Underwood said.

"I mean, it's amazing how some of these assholes make it through life, you know? How they make everyday decisions. And the chicks are even worse. Fuck!"

"I got my bags," Underwood said.

"You don't want to go to the bar?"

"Not here; let's leave. Let's get the fuck out of here, huh?"

"Why are you in such a hurry?"

"I just am," Underwood said.

"Where do you want to go then?" Reggie asked. "The house?"

"Yeah, I really want to see the house," Underwood said. "This huge fucking incredible house everyone keeps telling me about. I want to see it."

"Okay, okay," Reggie said.

Reggie grabbed one of Jack's bags and they headed out for the parking lot. Reggie popped the trunk and they put the bags in the car.

"It's been a long time, man" Reggie said.

"So, you still suck cock on film?" Underwood asked, and laughed.

"No, I quit doing that a while ago," Reggie said. "It's too bad. Real good money in fag stuff. But I was getting kind of scared, you know? Diseases, man."

"I know," Underwood said. "Shit, I don't know why you did that shit for as long as you did."

"The money."

"I know, but there's a limit?" Underwood said. "I mean, there's a line you can't cross, isn't there?"

"There didn't used to be. But now I'm older and I'm trying to be wiser. And I guess I care about things more now. When I was younger, I didn't give a fuck about anything, you know? Just the green."

"I tried doing that shit once. But I had to leave the set in the middle of a scene. I just went into the bathroom and threw up for fifteen minutes. Then I just left. Fuck that. No dollar amount on that, man."

"You just didn't have the stomach for it."

"You got that right," Underwood said. "It ain't my scene, and I can't fake it."

"Well, you do all right otherwise, don't you?"

"I got money in the bank," Underwood said. "I do okay."

"Remember the old days, man?" Reggie said. "We had some wild times."

"Lot of the people we started out with moved on to other stuff. We're a dying breed, Reg."

"A dying breed."

"So is this house really so fucking incredible?"

"You'll see," Reggie said. They were just driving out of the airport parking lot, getting onto the highway.

"You didn't tell anyone I was coming early, did you?"

"Me?" Reggie said. "No, I didn't tell anyone. Not even Tony. But don't worry, there's plenty of room. You won't have to sleep on no floors."

"I wasn't planning to," Underwood said.

"You sure you don't want to stop at a bar on the way?"

"No," Underwood said. "I want to get settled in. Drop off my bags and stretch my legs, you know?"

"Okay. There's plenty of booze at the house anyway."

"Got any blow?"

"Man, it's like a blizzard in there. Anything you want."

"Cool. Hey, you know that young bitch Lilac? She there yet?"

"Yeah, she's there."

"We had a scene together in the last movie I worked on."

"She's got this new guy with her, some kind of boyfriend. He's as old as we are. You'd think Tony would want some young stud or something."

"Yeah," Underwood said. "But there's something to be said for us older guys, huh?"

"A dying breed, man."

CHAPTER 69

They started out playfully enough, helping each other get undressed. They were actually laughing as they dropped their clothes on the floor. Then Francie made Ariadne stretch out on the bed, and they kissed. Ariadne couldn't get over how soft Francie's lips were. After they had been kissing awhile, Francie moved down, kissing Ariadne's body in multiple places as she traveled.

She lingered on Ariadne's breasts, teasing her nipples with her tongue. Then she was on the move again.

Instead of lying back, Ariadne was propped up on her elbows, watching as Francie licked her thighs. She wanted to watch.

"What are you looking at?" Francie wanted to know.

"You. I want to see what you're doing."

"Well then, I guess I have to give you something to watch."

Francie's face went between Ariadne's legs, as she used her tongue and her lips, and then her fingers. Eventually, Ariadne stopped watching and stretched back down again. She focused on what Francie was making her feel.

It didn't take long for the orgasm to happen. Maybe it was the thrill of doing something she never thought she would do before, or maybe Francie was just really good at what she did. But Ariadne squirmed in delight.

"Don't stop," she said, opening her eyes again to stare up at the ceiling. "Don't."

"No," Francie said. "I won't be stopping anytime soon."

When Ariadne stopped squirming so much, Francie got up on the bed and positioned her body above Ariadne's mouth.

"Now it's your turn," Francie said.

"Tell me if I'm doing this right," Ariadne said, and grabbed her friend's pelvis, pulling it down toward her.

Francie continued to work on Ariadne. Licking her clitoris, putting two and then three fingers inside her. And, at the other end, Ariadne was doing the same to her.

Their bodies entwined like hungry vines, as they took turns making each other come.

CHAPTER 70

"Don't be nervous," Lilac said.

Merry mumbled something and followed her out of the dressing room and onto the set, one of the house's many bedrooms. A big canopy bed was the centerpiece.

Lilac was dressed like a French maid. She was always role-playing. It had something to do with the fact that she looked so young. They always wanted her to dress like schoolgirls and candy stripers. She liked it, too—she'd told him once, when they'd been wrapped up in each other, after a long lovemaking session. She said the outfits were a real turn-on.

He watched her ass as she moved in front of him. Not for the first time, he thought, *How the hell am I going to keep up with her? It's only a matter of time before I lag behind and she loses interest.*

But this wasn't the right time to be thinking about that. This was time to perform. Time to jump through the flaming hoop. Time to dazzle them with his stamina. There was going to be an audience, and he was expected to put on a show.

When he first agreed to do it, he thought it would be fun. He had never done anything like this before. But then, Phil got into his head, and it just got worse from there. Merry was determined not to back out, but the anticipation had been making him miserable. Lilac obviously noticed. Now was the time to make it up to her.

"Hey, Merry," Tony said from behind the glaring lights. "You going to leave that key around your neck?"

It was like his security blanket. He wasn't going to give it up now. "It's just a short chain," he said.

"Okay," Tony said, letting it go. "Let's set up the scene.

Merry, you're a guest in this fancy mansion. You've just gone to bed and the maid comes in. She says she has to do some cleaning. Ready?"

Lilac looked at Merry and then back at Tony. "We're ready."

"Great," Tony said. "Let's go."

Lilac went into the hallway.

Merry sat on the canopy bed in his clothes. He tried not to look at the cameras. There was a knock at the door.

"Who is it?" Merry asked.

"It is ze maid, Monsieur," Lilac said from behind the door, trying her best to sound French. Not that the audience for these kinds of films would care about authenticity.

Merry got up and opened the door. Lilac stood there with her hands on her hips.

"So sorry to bother you," she said. "But I must clean ze room."

"It's too late to be cleaning up."

She tried to move past him, and he stepped aside. It was a brief moment of awkwardness that would have been funny if he wasn't so determined to prove himself. She closed the door.

"I have my orders, Monsieur."

"Okay, okay," he said, and went back to the bed. He sat down and watched her as she dusted with a large feather brush.

Her skirt was very short, and he watched her ass as she cleaned. She wasn't wearing panties. He knew the cameras were focusing on that, too. That perfect ass.

She turned to look at him. "Monsieur," she said, "you seem so tense. Would you like a massage?"

Merry smiled. "Sure."

"Take off your clothes, please," she said. "So that I may do it properly."

It wasn't great acting, but Merry wasn't under the impression he'd been hired to act. He was hired to fuck, and that's what he planned on doing. He started taking off his shirt. Lilac rushed over to help. Soon they were kissing. Deep, soul kisses, and he was undressing her as well. She started out massaging him. He was on his stomach and she was naked, on top of him, rubbing his back and shoulders with her whole body.

"Turn over, please," she said, and he did.

She climbed on top of him and slid down on his cock. With the hot lights and cameras he thought he'd freeze. He worried about keeping it up, but now, with her on top of him, moving up and down, he found that he could block those things out. She kept him focused on *her*, and he was happy to oblige. When he looked up into her face, all he wanted to do was make her come.

He closed his eyes and tried to think about baseball instant replays and boxing and boring news programs and anything else he could get his memory around that would prolong the thing and keep his dick hard. She was so wet, so wonderful, that it took all his effort to keep from coming. But he had to last. He had to go the distance.

They rolled around on the bed. It was almost turning into a wrestling match, it was that passionate. They changed positions, and he found himself man-handling her more than he did when they were alone. He was playing to the cameras and he didn't even realize it.

She rolled her eyes and started to moan. He couldn't tell if she was faking it, but it didn't matter. It was enough to focus his excitement.

He grabbed her and increased the momentum. The harder he thrust himself into her, the louder her noises got. He felt he'd accomplished something, that he'd won the fight with a TKO. And at that point, he couldn't hold it back anymore.

"I'm corning," he said.

She slid off and put her mouth on it. She looked so angelic, so loving, as he came on her face. He had wanted to come inside her, but Tony had told him they had to have the money shot.

As she licked up the last of it, Tony shouted, "Cut!"

Lilac sat up. "Well, you did it, Merry."

"Not bad for a first timer, Merry," Tony said. "That's a wrap."

In the corner, hidden in the shadows, Underwood watched them.

He's not so fucking great, Underwood thought. *I could fuck circles around that asshole.*

CHAPTER 71

"Ariadne?" Reynold said. "Are you there?" A moment later, he repeated "Ariadne? I suppose you aren't there. This is Reynold."

She grabbed the receiver, pulled it to her ear. "Hello?" she said before he could continue leaving a message. "Reynold? What's wrong?"

"Nothing's wrong. I just wanted to call. I know I gave you the week off, but I wanted to get together with you, maybe tomorrow for lunch? I think we should talk."

"Is this like a date?" she asked, wondering if he was interested in her too, like Mitch had been. She really didn't need any more complications.

"No," he said firmly. "This is all business."

"Okay. Lunch tomorrow. Where?"

"I'll have a driver pick you up around one thirty. Okay? I like to avoid the lunch crowds."

There was no point in prolonging this. She had made up her mind, and it would give her the chance to officially quit and be done with all this. "Fine," she said. "I'll be ready."

"It'll be nice, I promise you," he said.

"Sure," she said, trying to convince him she wasn't worried. Trying to convince *herself*.

"Great," Reynold said, hanging up.

For the first time in her life, she was terrified. Ariadne had always been in control, had always been tough and in charge. But now she felt helpless. She had no idea what Reynold had in mind for her, and the whole incident with Mitch had left her with doubts.

Was she in danger? Did they think she was in on whatever

scam Mitch had been operating? Was her life as expendable as Mitch's had been?

Reynold sounded like he was trying to put her mind at ease, but all she could picture in her head was being tied to a chair like Mitch had been, awaiting her own interrogation.

What's happened to me? she wondered. *Why am I so scared and feel so helpless?*

She felt a hand on her shoulder, and turned. Hard.

"Whoa!" Francie said. "Why so jumpy? Who was on the phone?"

"Work," Ariadne said.

"Man, you're shaking like a leaf," Francie said. "What's going on here?"

"Nothing," Ariadne said.

"Bullshit," Francie told her. "Look, we've always been able to talk to each other, haven't we? Why can't you talk to me about this? Ever since your last job, you've been acting weird. Nervous. I want you to tell me what happened, and why you're so afraid."

So she did.

CHAPTER 72

There was a party in the big ballroom downstairs.

It looked as if the whole porn industry was down there. Some of them were famous faces (and bodies) he had seen on video. It was almost like a Hollywood premiere. Lilac was talking with almost everyone. Merry kind of followed her as she worked the room, keeping up his end of the chatter with small talk.

At one point, Merry saw Jack Underwood. He tried to pretend he hadn't seen him, but Underwood moved through the crowd toward them.

"Here comes trouble," Merry whispered in Lilac's ear.

"Long time no see," Underwood said. He swept Lilac up in his arms and squeezed her, and then put her back down. He shook Merry's hand.

"How long have you been here?" Lilac asked.

"Just got here," Underwood said. "Seeing a lot of people I haven't seen in years, catching up on old times. This really is something, huh?"

"Yes it is!" Lilac said, sounding enthusiastic.

"Did you have your big scene yet?" Underwood asked, looking from Lilac to Merry.

"Yep, we did it," Merry said.

"Was Merry here able to keep it up?" Underwood said, nudging Merry in the ribs.

"He was great," Lilac said. "You never would have known it was his first time in front of the cameras."

"Hey, Merry, maybe you're a natural."

Merry grunted. He wanted to get as far away from Underwood as possible.

"How much longer are you here?" Underwood asked.

"I have a couple of girl-girl scenes tomorrow, and then we'll be going home."

"So soon?" Underwood said, seeming surprised. "Hell, you just got here. Why not stick around? This house is so huge, you could stay here forever and nobody would ever know. Tony's got about five crews going around to different rooms, shooting scenes. It's amazing, like an assembly line of fucking."

"Yeah, Tony told some of his buddies about it and they're shooting some films here too, before he has to clear the place out. It is pretty amazing," Lilac said.

"You going to have any more scenes, Merry?"

"I don't think so."

"Hey, I hear they're shooting some gay porn on the second floor. You should audition," Underwood said, enjoying Merry's discomfort.

"No thanks."

"Don't you want to try new things?"

Merry resisted the urge to throw a punch. It took some effort. "I guess I'm just not that adventurous."

"Too bad," Underwood said. "I think you'd be a natural."

"I think I see Chrissie over there," Lilac said. "Excuse us, will you?"

"Sure thing," he said. "Give Chrissie my best, will you?"

Underwood was going to tag along, just to make them miserable, but he could always fuck with them later on. He spotted Reggie doing coke on a long coffee table with some other old-timers.

He moved toward them. "Hey—got enough for one more?"

Everyone looked up, their noses flaked with white powder.

"Hey, it's Jack," Reggie said.

"Yep," he said, enjoying the attention. "Slide over, Reggie, and let the master show you a thing or two."

CHAPTER 73

A hostess escorted Ariadne to the back of the restaurant. Reynold was sitting at his table, sipping wine, and his eyes widened when she approached. He nodded for her to sit.

"Would you like something to drink?"

"I'll have what you're having," she said.

"Bring a bottle," Reynold told the waiter, who then left. Another man came over right away to fill their water glasses.

It was midday, and many of the other tables were vacant. They were far enough away from the ones that weren't to have a sense of privacy.

"I hope you don't mind my getting right to the point," Ariadne said. "But what business did you want to discuss?"

"Relax," Reynold said. "I told you this would be a nice, pleasant meal. Enjoy it."

The waiter came back with a bottle of wine and another glass for Ariadne. He opened the bottle for them and poured.

"Would you like to order?"

"Not yet," Reynold said.

The man left without another word.

She looked down at the menu. It all looked so good.

"I come here often. If you like, I could order for us both."

"That sounds fine," she said.

"Good, it'll be fun. I won't order anything awful, I promise." Reynold lifted his glass.

She hesitated and then lifted her own.

"To you," he said. "And the fine job you've been doing."

Ariadne hesitated again and then followed his lead and drank.

"No reason to keep you in suspense," he told her. "I'm here to woo you."

She stared at him, unsure of what to say.

"But not in the way you think. I want to woo you into staying with us. I don't want you to quit."

He took a long sip. "Don't tell me you haven't been doing a lot of thinking about it lately. I know you have. I know the whole thing with Mitch was a shock, and that it may have soured you on this occupation of yours. I want to tell you this was an anomaly, and a mistake. I never should have involved you. But I did because I wanted you to find out what kind of man he was. I didn't want him lying to you any longer."

"It's not just that. It's a lot of things. I just don't have the desire to keep doing this. It isn't in my blood anymore."

"Now you're lying to yourself. Once it's in your blood, it never leaves. To be capable of doing what you do takes a special kind of mind. And that doesn't just leave you one day. It's who you are. It's a special kind of sadism that you're born with. Please don't deny it."

She wasn't sure what she thought about his use of the word *sadism*, but she chose to ignore it. She drank from her glass and suddenly realized she'd already drained it.

He lifted the bottle. "Let me refill that."

She held her glass out.

"Maybe I didn't handle things right," he told her. "I should have been up front with you right away. Told you about the kinds of things Mitch was doing. But I wanted you to hear it from his own lips. I didn't think you'd just take my word for it. After all, you haven't known me for very long. And I haven't known you, although I've certainly been aware of you for quite a long time. You see, you're respected in our circles. You are capable and efficient at what you do."

"Thank you."

"Perhaps you haven't been told that before," he said. "Perhaps you had no idea how your work was being received."

"I was getting paid, and I was getting plenty of work. That was enough."

"No, that's not enough. Good work should be praised. Rewarded."

The waiter came back. Reynold read from the menu and looked at Ariadne every now and then and smiled. When he was done, the waiter left again.

"There is a pasta dish they serve here that is out of this world," he said. "You are going to love it. I want you to enjoy the meal. I've known women who were so obsessed with dieting that all food tastes bad to them. All food tastes like weakness. Not that you should ever worry about such things."

"I worry sometimes. I'm just like any other woman."

"No," he said. "There you are wrong."

She drained her glass again. He offered to refill it, but she put her hand over the glass, refusing.

"You are the strongest woman I have ever known," he said.

"I think you're confusing strength with the ability to inflict pain," she said. "They're two different things."

"Are they?" he asked. He smiled at her, sipped form his glass. "Promise me you'll really think about this before you make any kind of decision. That you won't act hastily."

"Okay," she said.

"And I promise you, no more surprises like the one with Mitch."

The waiter carne with soup. He placed the bowls before them and went away.

"One thing about Mitch," Reynold said. "It should teach you a lesson. Not to get involved with anyone you work with. Sometimes things get messy, and it's good to be able to protect yourself from any unnecessary pain."

He swallowed a spoonful of soup. "Although I can see why Mitch was so tempted."

She smiled. It was probably the wine. She asked him for another refill after all.

"Make no mistake," he said softly, looking into her eyes, "if you were involved in Mitch's dealings, if you were an accomplice, you wouldn't be here right now. But we know you're loyal. And we are, in turn, loyal to you."

She felt a chill, despite the wine. Was that some kind of a veiled threat? How were they so *sure* she was loyal? Did they have someone watching her?

He had been talking seriously, but then he smiled again. "I'm so glad we can trust you. I would hate to see anything happen to you. Ever."

"Is all this your way of telling me I'm not allowed to quit?" It had been on her mind since the start, and she felt relieved to have said it aloud.

"Think about it," he told her. "Take as long as you want. If you need more time off, take it. You can have two weeks, three weeks. But think about it. Carefully."

"I will," she said.

"I think a person should do what's best for herself. If you feel you need a change, then perhaps it's for the best. But some of my superiors have old-fashioned ideas. Some of them may see your quitting as an act of disloyalty."

That's a threat, alright, she thought.

The waiter came and took their bowls. Ariadne had only finished about half her soup. Then he placed dishes in front of them. Pasta in a white cheese sauce with chunks of lobster.

He bowed and was off again.

"Like I said," Reynold said. "Some of them may see it as a kind of disloyalty, but then again, maybe not. Maybe they are as open-minded as I try to be. I can't be sure."

He looked over at her.

She was staring at him. She was not eating.

"Try some, it's wonderful," he said. "Mangia, mangia!"

She looked down at the food. It looked wonderful, but her appetite was pretty much gone. It took some effort to force some of it down.

They ate in relative silence, and when she'd finished what she could, she excused herself and went out to the waiting car, which took her home.

CHAPTER 74

Merry had gone a little overboard with the drinking, that was obvious. He had never been one for parties and had attempted to dispel some of his anxiety with two-fisted consumption. He tried to remember if he did anything the previous night that he should regret—something in the back of his mind told him this could be a possibility—but he came up blank. Lilac wasn't in the room, but then she had to do some filming today and was probably working.

By the time he got dressed, Lilac was still nowhere around. Had she said anything else? He remembered that bastard Underwood. That guy really got under his skin. Maybe he'd gotten drunk and thrown a punch at him. It didn't sound right. He didn't have any marks on him, and Underwood would definitely have fought back.

Merry decided to go exploring. They'd been in this house for three days now, and he hadn't really looked around on his own. He'd spent most of the time with Lilac, going where she'd wanted to go.

He entered the huge, cavernous hallway. The walls were covered with bright red fabric. He picked a direction and walked. Most of the doors were closed, but a couple were open.

Merry looked in one of the rooms. They were filming a scene where about six guys were standing around a girl. She was on her knees and they were jerking off on her.

He kept walking down the hall.

What little he could remember of the night before convinced him that the party had degenerated into a full-on orgy. Not that that was surprising, with a house full of porn stars. He just wished he could remember it more clearly, so he could enjoy it. But something else was bothering him, something he couldn't get a handle on.

"Hey, buddy, come here." a guy said as he passed one room.

"Yeah?"

"Come in here," the guy said. Merry had never seen him before. "Are you in the middle of something?"

"No," Merry said.

The man led Merry inside. There were cameras and lights already set up to shoot a scene. "How'd you like to help us out, pal?"

Another guy, presumably the director, walked over to them.

"One of the guys we needed for this shoot didn't show up," the director said. "He's probably sleeping it off somewhere, but I don't have a clue where anyone is staying, and we can't find him. How'd you like to fill in?"

"I don't know."

"What's with the hesitating, that's why you're here, right?"

Merry was still a little foggy. "What do I have to do?"

"Just fuck the Princess over there, that's all."

Merry looked over to where the director pointed. Standing in a doorway, talking to a makeup person, was the most beautiful girl he had ever seen. She was Japanese, dressed in royal-looking, silken robes.

Her heavily made-up eyes rested on him for a moment. She smiled.

She looked familiar. He knew he had never met her before, but he was sure he had seen her in a movie.

"How's about it?" the director asked.

He thought about it. Lilac was off doing who knew what. And if she was going to do a little more work, why shouldn't he? And "the Princess," as they'd called her, was so damned beautiful.

"I think I can handle that."

"Of course you can," the director said. "Go get some makeup."

Merry walked over to where the Princess was standing.

"Hello," she said. "Are you in this scene?"

"I am now," Merry said with a stupid grin on his face. He turned to the makeup woman. "I'm supposed to get made up."

"Sure," the woman said. "Come over here."

The Princess squeezed his ass as he moved past her.

Merry took off his clothes and put them on a chair. The makeup woman started touching him up with brushes. The Princess stood in the doorway, watching him.

She sure seemed friendly enough, Merry thought. The Princess smiled and licked her lips when she saw Merry looking her way, and then she left.

In the bedroom, they'd removed the bed and replaced it with some kind of throne. It didn't look too bad, although, on closer look, it was obvious it had been thrown together quickly using what they could find around the house. The Princess took her place on the throne and waited for her cue.

The director came in while Merry was getting ready.

"Listen, you don't need any lines or anything. Here's what's happening, okay? You're a prisoner in this land of warrior women, and the Princess there is their queen. Two female soldiers are going to throw you down in front of her, and from then on just do what she says. Okay?"

"Sure," Merry said.

"Great," the director said. "Thanks for helping us out."

He left the room. Merry put on a tunic the costumer handed to him. Two women dressed like soldiers stood near the door now, waiting for him. They were both topless, with enormous breasts, and each wore an extravagant, feathered headdress.

It was the fanciest porn set he'd ever seen. He approached them. Each one grabbed one of his arms.

"Action!" the director called out.

The Princess was dressed in a long robe that had fallen open. She was naked underneath. She had a large black dildo and began to fuck it on the throne. Merry watched as she got more and more excited. When she started moaning, the director waved for them to enter.

The female soldiers pulled him toward the throne, and once they got there, they made him kneel before it.

The Princess was still playing with herself, bringing herself to orgasm (or pretending to), and was oblivious to them.

When she quieted down, one of the female soldiers cleared her throat.

"What would you like us to do to this prisoner, Your Majesty?" the soldier asked.

The Princess looked Merry over.

"Stand before me," she said.

The women soldiers forced him to his feet.

"Strip this slave," the Princess said.

One of the soldiers pulled off Merry's tunic, and the Princess smiled.

"I have special plans for this one."

Merry tried to look up at her.

"Keep your head down, slave," one of the soldiers said. "You shall not look upon the Princess until she allows it."

He obeyed, trying to stay in character. The lights were making his hangover throb, but he tried to ignore it.

"Go, now," the Princess said clapping her hands, and the soldiers left.

She reached down and caressed his face. He looked up at her.

"You belong to me now, slave," she said. "Do you know what I will do with you?"

Merry said nothing. He just looked up at the beautiful face.

"Take off my robe!" she demanded.

Merry rose to his feet and undressed her. She then got down on her knees and started sucking his dick. In no time, they were on the floor, using their mouths on each other. He always thought it was funny when people said they didn't want to have sex because they had a headache. It was a joke as old as the hills. "Sorry, honey, I have a headache." He thought it was funny because sex always seemed to *ease* his headaches. Maybe it wasn't the same for everyone, but, in his case, a headache was a great reason to have sex.

The throbbing in his head subsided as he rolled around with the Princess. If his sex scene the day before with Lilac had seemed like wrestling part of the time, this scene was even more like it. The Princess turned herself around and pinned him to the ground as she climbed on top of him, grabbing his dick and shoving it inside her. It was like she was determined to fuck him, not the other way around. He was so caught up in it that he didn't even notice the camera and the lights. He really got into it.

At one point, as he was on top of her, slamming away at her, he thought he saw Lilac come into the room out of the corner of his eye, watch him, and leave hurriedly. But he couldn't be sure it was her. It could have been anyone. And he couldn't stop, not then. He was almost about to come. He made sure to come on the Princess's belly.

When the scene was over, the director yelled "Cut," and Merry got to his feet. He helped the Princess to hers, too. He looked around the room, but didn't see any sign of Lilac. The director had moved to another part of the big room, where the two female soldiers were now going down on each other.

He went back to the dressing room and put his clothes back on. The guy who had talked to him in the hallway came in and gave him some cash. He put it in his pocket.

"You really saved us some time and money," the man said.

"Thanks," Merry said.

"That was a blast," the Princess said, coming into the room as he was leaving.

"Yeah, it was fun."

"Let's do it again sometime."

"Sure," he said.

She leaned forward and kissed him.

He left, moving around the lights and the cameras and returned to the hallway. He felt pretty good about himself at that moment.

Then he remembered the girl who had come in and watched him.

Had it been Lilac?

He tried to find his way back to their room. There were so many doors and they all looked the same.

He entered one room that he thought was theirs, and another movie was being filmed in there. A girl was getting fucked by two men. They both had their cocks in her vagina and were pumping away. The girl was shouting in pleasure.

He continued down the hall, trying to figure out where his room was.

CHAPTER 75

"How did it go?" Francie asked when Ariadne got back.

"Well, he let me know that if I quit, I might end up dead," Ariadne said.

"He said that?"

"He didn't have to come right out and say it. But he made himself very clear."

"What are you going to do?" Francie asked.

"I have no fucking idea. Somehow, I've lost the ability to make choices for myself. Reynold and the people he works for call the shots now."

"Then maybe you'd better not quit."

"Don't worry, I'll figure a way out of this." She seemed to brighten a little. "I've been in tough spots before. I'll get the angle on this one."

"How?"

"Let me worry about that. He told me I can think about it for as long as I need, and I plan to take advantage of that time to think of a plan."

"Don't do anything crazy."

"Don't worry so much."

"I finally get you to myself, and they're going to take you away."

"No one is taking me anywhere," Ariadne said. "Hey, let's get our minds off this. Since I'm already dressed up anyway, let's go out. Go put on something special and let's get out of here. I want to go dancing."

CHAPTER 76

When Merry found the room again, it was still empty. He knew it was the right room when he saw their suitcases. *Maybe it wasn't her*, he thought.

He decided to take a shower and then go looking for her again.

While he was in the shower, Lilac came back. He heard her slamming things in the bedroom.

He was about to get out of the shower when she came in.

"You son of a bitch!"

"Lilac," he said. "What's wrong?"

"I saw you fucking her!" she said. "Don't try to lie to me."

"I won't," Merry said. "Just let's talk calmly about this."

"I can't believe you could just forget me like that."

"What? I was wandering around looking for you, and some guy asked if I could do a scene. I didn't think it mattered. I mean, you were doing scenes without me, having sex with other people."

"We had a deal, Merry," she said, her face red with anger. "Or don't you remember?"

"I'm a little fuzzy there," Merry said. "I woke up with one helluva hangover."

"I'm not surprised, the way you were drinking last night," she said. "We had a deal Merry. I wouldn't fuck any other guys and you wouldn't fuck any girls. We had a *commitment*, Merry."

"I'm sorry," he said. "I wasn't thinking. Some guy asked me to be in a movie and I just went along with it. I didn't mean anything by it. You know what this place is like."

"I was looking for you, and there you were with that bitch, fucking on the floor."

"It was for a movie!"

"That bitch! It was bad enough she was coming on to you last night. You practically balled her right in front of me. Don't you remember?"

"No! I really don't." But the Princess *had* looked familiar. And something had been nagging him about last night. "I don't remember anything, I swear."

"Fuck off," Lilac said, and left, slamming the bathroom door.

He stood there, under the running water, not sure what to do. Eventually, he shut the water off and went out into the bedroom, wanting to apologize.

Lilac was already gone. So was her suitcase.

CHAPTER 77

Merry wandered around the mansion for hours. There were so many rooms, searching for her seemed to take forever.

He collapsed near the pool on one of the sun chairs. He had no idea where else to go, but he wanted to rest for a couple of minutes.

"Hi there," a woman said.

He turned. It was the Princess.

She smiled. "Mind if I join you?"

"I'm not staying long," he said. "I have to find Lilac. Do you know her?"

"I've met her," she said. She wasn't wearing the robes or the heavy eye makeup anymore, but she was still the most gorgeous woman he had ever seen. Looking at her almost took his breath away. Then he thought of Lilac. He belonged with *her* right now.

"Have you seen her?"

"Not since last night."

Merry had no desire to ask her real name. "The Princess" suited her.

"Since we're right here by the pool, how's about we go skinny dipping?"

He got up from his chair. "I've really got to find Lilac."

She rubbed up close to him. "You know, I can make you forget all about her. That bit we did this afternoon, that was just a taste, baby."

He didn't doubt it, but he thought of Lilac. "I have to go."

She put her arms around him. "Come on, honey. Give me a chance to change your mind!"

He pushed her away. "Nothing personal. I had a great time

at that shoot. But I really have to find Lilac."

"Suit yourself. I don't beg."

Merry walked around her and went back inside the house and headed toward the stairs.

"Hey, you looking for Lilac?" someone said.

It was Reggie. Merry had met him the night before. He'd seemed okay.

"Yeah," Merry said. "Do you know where she is?"

"She left a little while ago, man," Reggie said. "Left with Jack. Jack Underwood."

"Are you sure?"

"Of course I'm sure."

"Where'd they go? Down to the beach?"

"I don't have a clue where they went, man," Reggie said. "I thought I heard her say something about wanting to go home. But who knows where they went off to?"

"You're shitting me. You mean home as in going to the airport?"

"That's what she said, man. She had her suitcase with her and everything. All I know is Jack told me he was splitting, and to tell Tony. Then they took off. Tony is gonna be livid."

Reggie walked away.

Merry stood there, frozen. Not sure what to do.

He had to find Lilac and apologize. Make her understand. He couldn't let it end like this.

And most of all, there was *no way in hell* he was going to let Jack Underwood steal her away.

CHAPTER 78

❝Can you imagine the look on Merry's face right now? He must be shitting a brick!" Underwood said.

Lilac was half-conscious. She grunted a reply.

"Not only did you take off on him," he said, with a laugh, "but you left with *me*. Shit! It's going to mess him up good. I made sure Reggie told him after we'd been gone a while. I'll bet he told him by now, I just wish I could see his face. I love to fuck with that guy"

Lilac tried to focus. If she'd been able to, she might have had a change of heart about all this. She might have wanted to try to patch things up with Merry. But right now, she wasn't even fully sure who Merry was. Underwood had given her some pills on the ride to the airport, and they had packed a much bigger wallop than she had expected. It took all her energy just to keep her eyes open.

"You know, I thought you didn't have any taste at all," Underwood said. "Going for a loser like Merry. But baby, I take it all back. Your leaving with me restored my faith in you."

Lilac grunted. She stared out the window of the plane. It was night, and she could see lights below, but had no idea what was below them.

"Wait till we get back," Underwood said. "I'll show you how a real man makes love. And it won't be no fake movie shit, either. I'll do you for real. Your head will be spinning."

Her head was *already* spinning.

"Do you think Merry will come looking for you? Or do you think he'll just give up now that the better man has won? I'll tell you, I hope he *does* come looking. I'll kick his ass right in front of you, show him who's boss."

Lilac felt some drool on her lip, but she couldn't feel her hands to wipe it away. She didn't remember much of the ride up, or boarding the plane. Weren't they supposed to refuse passengers who were too drunk to fly? Hadn't anyone noticed how out of it she was?

"You're so quiet," Underwood said. "Shit, don't tell me you're shy around a real man like me. You really don't know what treats I've got in store for you, girlie."

Lilac turned to face him. She noticed that her seatbelt was fastened.

"Don't worry, Lilac. When we get back, I'll make you forget all about that guy. I can't wait to give you my sweet love, baby. Unless you can't wait and you want to join the Mile High Club, or are you already a member?"

Lilac watched some lights spinning in front of her eyes.

CHAPTER 79

It was late, and Ariadne rolled over in bed and found herself alone.

She thought she had heard voices, so she slipped out of bed and quietly opened the door. She moved through the hall until she spotted Francie. Francie did not see her; she had her back to her, and was talking on the phone, trying to keep her voice down.

Who would she be talking to at this hour? Ariadne wondered.

She retreated back down the hall without making a sound and went back into the bedroom, where there was a second phone. She very quietly picked it up and brought it to her ear.

"So is she still intent on quitting?" a man's voice said.

Ariadne recognized it immediately. It was Reynold.

"I've been trying to convince her not to quit," Francie said, barely above a whisper. "That it might be dangerous."

"Good," Reynold said. "Reinforce that in her mind. It's true, after all. And you wouldn't want anything to happen to her, now would you? Now that everything seems to be going your way?"

"I'll do my best."

"Sure you will," Reynold said. "You always do. She doesn't know how good you've been looking after her, does she?"

"No, of course not."

"Funny. You're like her guardian angel, watching over her. It's because of you that we knew she wasn't part of the whole scam with Mitch. That we knew we could still trust her. And she trusts you still?"

"Implicitly."

"And she has no idea? None at all?"

"None."

"Well, keep up the good work, and convince her to stay with us. We'd really hate to lose her."

"I'll take care of it."

"I'll be calling her at the end of the week to make sure she's staying. So get to work."

"I will," Francie said.

Reynold hung up. Francie sighed and hung up as well.

Ariadne replaced the phone softly and got under the sheets. She closed her eyes and thought about how she would handle things.

CHAPTER 80

After getting off the plane and collecting his luggage, Merry took a cab home.

He had no idea if Underwood and Lilac would be coming back here. For all he knew, they could be anywhere.

The answering machine was flashing. He pushed the button and paced the room, hoping one was from Lilac.

"Where the hell are you?" a man's voice asked. "I wanna see that cock of yours. Come over to the window and show it to me."

"I don't believe it," Merry said. "I don't fucking believe it!"

The next message was also from his admirer across the way.

"Why don't you come over and fuck that girl of yours over here, so I can watch your dick slide in and out of her ass."

The guy's voice was breathy, labored, like he was pulling his cock as he spoke. He probably *was*.

There were three other messages from him. They got progressively worse. This was a guy with a lot of time on his hands and not much to do.

There was anger inside Merry. Anger at Lilac for leaving him like that. Anger at Underwood for taking her away. That bastard was probably laughing at him the whole time. Now he felt anger toward this obscene phone caller asshole who had been tormenting him for weeks.

Anger became fury.

He had held it in long enough. This stuff was like pressure, cooking inside him, and it had to be released somewhere.

Merry left the apartment and walked across the courtyard that separated their buildings. It was late, but some kids were hanging out on the steps.

Merry had brought his gun, and it was tucked in behind his belt.

"One of you live in this building?"

"Yeah," one of the kids said. About sixteen. Sucking down a beer.

"I'm here to see someone, but I want to surprise him. Can you let me in?"

"Sure," the kid said. "But it'll cost you."

Merry wasn't in the mood to haggle. He pulled out his wallet, gave the kid a twenty.

"Can you show me the way?" Merry asked.

"You want an escort, huh?"

"Yep."

"Okay." The kid led him to the front door. Merry did not want to tip Finch off. And he knew it was going to be hard to get the drop on him again.

The kid took out his key and opened the door.

"Who you wanna see?"

"Guy named Jay," Merry said. "Jay Finch."

"For some reason I thought he'd be the one," the kid said. "You got a beef with him?"

"Nah, I'm an old friend, just come to say hi."

"Okay, follow me." The kid led him up the stairs to the third floor. They stopped in front of the door.

"Knock on it," Merry whispered. "Tell him it's you."

The kid knocked on the door. It was late, so it took a few tries.

"Who is it?" a voice asked from the other side.

"It's Jerry," the kid said.

"What do you want at this hour?"

The kid looked at Merry. "I need some money," Jerry said. "Let me in, man."

"You thought about what I said," Finch asked from behind the door. "You changed your mind, huh?"

The kid looked nervous. "Yeah, Mr. Finch. I really need that money."

"I was wondering when you'd come around, kid," Finch said.

The kid was standing in front of the door. He looked scared. He moved as if he was about to run, but Merry grabbed his arm.

"Come on in, Jerry," Finch said, as he unlocked the door and opened it.

Merry let go of the kid's arm. Jerry took off down the stairs.

"Jerry?" Finch asked, coming out into the hallway. One of his arms was in a sling.

Merry moved forward and grabbed Finch's arms, pushing him inside. Then he kicked the door closed.

"You!" the man said, looking angry and terrified. "What the fuck are you doing here?"

"Don't you remember?" Merry asked. "You left me a message, five of them in fact, inviting me over. So you can see my big cock in action."

"Get out of here!"

"I thought I'd be a little more subtle this time, coming to see you," Merry said. "Heaven knows *you* could be more subtle. But it just isn't in you, is it?"

"I have a gun," Finch said. "And your father isn't here to protect you this time."

"Protect me? Listen, that gun of yours won't do you any good if you can't use it, asshole. And me, I've come prepared. I'm sick of you and your fucking phone calls. This is where I teach you a lesson on manners."

Merry punched the man full in the face. Finch dropped to his knees.

Merry kicked him, holding the man's arm so he couldn't fall. "I don't want any more phone calls," Merry said. "I want you to keep your lousy fucking voice out of my life. You got it?"

The man struggled. Merry punched him again, knocking him to the floor. "You got the message yet?"

The man didn't answer, so Merry hit him again. A fist to the jaw.

There was blood.

"You know, I've been wanting to do this for a long time. My father stopped me last time. But this time, you're going to get what's coming to you."

Merry grabbed Finch's face, made him look up at him. "Why

me?" Merry asked. "Why harass me?"

"I can't help it," the man said.

"Bullshit!"

"You've got to believe me," Jay Finch said. "I'm sick. I can't help myself."

"Well, maybe this will help," Merry said, and hit him again. The man grunted.

"I'm going to get an unlisted number," Merry said. He lifted the man to his feet and hit him one last time, so that he was sprawled on the floor.

"If you ever bother me again, your next lesson will be more permanent."

The man covered his bloody face with his hands and sobbed.

"Good-bye, Mr. Finch," Merry said. "I really don't expect to hear from you again."

Merry picked up a discarded shirt off the floor and wiped his bloody hands.

Finch was quiet as Merry got up and walked over to the door and let himself out.

Downstairs, the kids were still hanging out, drinking beer.

Jerry looked at Merry's hands.

"Did you hurt him, mister?" he asked.

"He got what was coming to him," Merry said.

"I'm glad," one of the other kids said.

Merry kept on walking.

CHAPTER 81

"I want to play a game," Ariadne said.

It was early in the morning, and she'd woken Francie with touches and kisses. Francie stirred, half-conscious.

"What?"

"Wake up," Ariadne said. "I want to have some fun."

She kissed Francie deeply, drawing her out of her slumber.

"Oooh," Francie said.

"I want to tie you up," Ariadne said.

Francie grunted.

"Stretch yourself out," Ariadne said, slipping off the bed.

"You're so kinky," Francie said, rubbing her eyes. "What a great way to wake up in the morning!"

Ariadne grabbed some scarves from her bureau and started tying Francie to the bedposts. "Now your legs," Ariadne said.

Francie laughed and stretched out her legs.

"Now you're helpless," Ariadne said.

"What are you going to do to me?"

Ariadne smiled. She leaned over and kissed Francie again. Long and slow. Then she ran her tongue down Francie's neck. Then down to her breasts. Her tongue lingered for a while and then traveled slowly down to her navel. She inserted her tongue there.

"Oh, baby!" Francie said. "You're one fast learner!"

Ariadne ran her tongue lower. Francie's thighs quivered.

Ariadne used her fingers and tongue. Francie wriggled in her bonds.

"Oh, God!" Francie said, trying to wiggle free. But the scarves held her tight.

"Shit!" she said. It was soft—like her voice had been on the phone the night before.

"I'm going to come," Francie said, not much later. "Oooh. You're so good at this. I told you you'd be a natural."

Ariadne didn't answer. She kept working away at Francie.

Francie's sounds grew less and less coherent.

When she was done, Ariadne slid off the bed and stood up.

"Oh, fuck, baby," Francie said. "That was amazing."

"I'm glad," Ariadne said.

"I love you, baby."

Ariadne stood there, looking at her.

"You can untie me now," Francie said. "So I can do you. "

Ariadne didn't move.

"Ari, please, take them off. They hurt. Please take them off."

"No."

"Come on," Francie said. "I don't like this game anymore."

"Do you love me?" Ariadne asked. "Really love me?"

"Of course I do, baby," Francie said. "I want to show you so badly."

"I hope you love me," Ariadne said. "Because if you do, I won't have to hurt you."

"Hurt me?" Francie said. "What are you talking about? You don't want to hurt me, do you? Why don't you let me go and I'll show you *how much* I love you."

"No, I have a better idea. I'm going to ask you some questions, and if you love me, you'll answer them honestly."

"What are you talking about, baby?"

"Enough of that 'baby' shit, okay? I'm serious. Are you ready for the first question?"

"You don't have to do this," Francie said. "I'll answer anything you ask me, baby. Really, I will."

"That's great to hear," Ariadne said. "How long have you known Reynold?"

Francie licked her lips. When she struggled against the scarves, it was obvious that it was causing her pain, so she stopped. She lay very still. "I don't know him," Francie said. "I only know what you've told me about him."

"You know, I wanted to give you some pleasure first. For

old times' sake. To show you how much your friendship has meant to me over the years. To show you I'm someone you can be honest with. Someone who wants to make you happy. But now you have to make *me* happy. You have to come clean."

"Really," Francie said. "I don't know what you're talking about."

"Maybe you're afraid of him," Ariadne said. "What he'll do to you if he finds out you've told me. But you see, he isn't here now. *I am*. And I'm just as dangerous as he is. In fact, right now, I'm *more* dangerous."

"I really wish you'd believe me," Francie said. "I don't know that guy. Really. You don't have to hurt me."

"Tell me the truth."

"Please untie me."

"No," Ariadne said. "Not until you tell me the truth."

"I told you."

"Okay." She knelt down and got something from under the bed. It was her black bag. She placed it on the bed and unzipped it. "I gave you your chance."

Francie struggled again. Her wrists and ankles were bleeding, but Ariadne was sure that the knots would hold.

"Stop it. You can't get away. You'll only hurt yourself more."

"Ariadne," Francie said. "What are you doing down there?"

"I thought you loved me," Ariadne said. "But that was just bullshit, wasn't it? I listened to you on the phone last night. I heard your conversation with Reynold."

"No."

"You lied to me just now," Ariadne said. "And people who love you don't lie to you. People who love you don't *spy* on you for someone else."

Ariadne took an electric drill out of her bag. She plugged it in a wall socket near the bed. When she pressed the trigger, the drill bit spun and the power tool squealed.

"No, Ariadne, you wouldn't," Francie said. "I'll tell you everything."

"Of course you will," Ariadne said. "But, you see, I gave you your chance, and you blew it. It could have just been pleasure, but you lied to me. Now I have to give you some pain."

"No, Ariadne!" Francie pleaded. "Don't do this!"

"I don't normally bring my work home with me, Francie. But it's about time you got to see what I do first hand."

CHAPTER 82

The light came on. Underwood was sitting up in bed, no doubt trying to determine where the noise had come from. The noise Merry had made to wake him. Merry was sitting in a chair near the wall switch.

He was holding a gun.

"Merry?" Underwood said. "Is that you?"

"You guessed it."

"How did you get in?"

"Where's Lilac?"

"Hey, you didn't answer my question."

"Fuck your question. They told me Lilac left with you. I want to talk to her."

"She ain't here," Underwood said. "As you can see, I'm alone. Somebody got their facts mixed up, buddy. Now I really need some sleep. You gotta go."

"I'm not going anywhere until I talk to Lilac."

"You hard of hearing?"

"I know she left with you. And I know damned well she would not have gone with you willingly. She hated you."

Underwood smiled. He seemed to be enjoying this. "You're such an asshole."

"I heard you tell Tony you were selling your parents' home and you were living here for the time being," Merry said. "I looked up your old address in our high school yearbook. So this is where you grew up, huh? Did you know I was here once, as a kid? It was a party after we graduated. I'd been jumping to a few different parties throughout the night, and I had no idea who lived here. I wasn't here long, so chances are you didn't even see me. But it's nice to see this place again, to see you here. Saves me having to go looking for you."

"You're out of your mind," Underwood said.

"Look, I'm not fucking around. I'll use this gun if I have to."

"This is against the law. Have you thought of that? You're committing a crime, breaking in here and threatening me. Or didn't they teach you that when you went to cop school? But I'll let it slide, for old times' sake. You just get on out now and I'll forget all about it."

"I'm not going anywhere," Merry said. "Tell me where Lilac is."

Underwood stared at him for a minute, and didn't say a word. Then he started laughing.

"What's so funny?"

"Okay, okay, you got me."

"Well?"

"Yeah, I flew back with Lilac. I admit it. Man, I was trying to spare you some heartache."

"What are you talking about?"

"She ditched you, man. And she took off with me. I don't want to rub it in.

"You're so concerned," Merry said. "It's moving."

"Man, I felt bad about it."

"But you did it, didn't you?"

"Yeah, I did," Underwood said. He was sitting up in bed, smiling. It was clear he didn't believe Merry would use the gun. Or maybe he just didn't care.

"Hey, if that girl hates me like you said, she sure has a weird way of showing it. She made sounds I'd never heard a bitch make before in that airplane bathroom."

Merry made sure no emotion crossed his face. "Where is she?"

"I don't know. But she isn't here, obviously."

Merry aimed the gun at his head. "Listen, jerkoff, I don't have time for this bullshit."

"Lighten up, will you? No need to do anything rash. She left me, too. Took off on me at the airport and took another plane out. She didn't say where, and I didn't ask where she was going."

"Bullshit. Why would she come all the way here, just to take another flight out again?"

"I don't know. Maybe it was a last minute decision. I don't claim to understand women sometimes, you know?" Underwood looked on the verge of laughing again.

"You are one stupid fuck, Underwood," Merry said. "Here I am, sitting here with a gun, and you're doing a stand-up act."

"You don't think I'm taking you seriously, do you? Look, you were a pussy in high school, and you're a pussy now. I mean, you couldn't even hack it as a cop. Trying to pretend you were a man I bet, walking around in some uniform, and you couldn't handle it. Shit, I could kick your ass then, and if you put that gun away, I'll kick it now."

"Where the fuck is Lilac?"

"I told you, already," Underwood said. "Look, this is getting tiresome, and I want to go back to sleep. "

"I don't believe you."

"So shoot me, you fucking idiot," Underwood said. He wasn't smiling anymore. "This is getting tired real fucking fast. I want you out of my house. Now."

"I'm not leaving until you tell me where Lilac is. Where she *really* is. I don't believe a word you say about her taking another flight."

"I don't care what you believe."

Merry stared at him. The guy talked and acted like *he* was in control. He was so sure that Merry wasn't going to follow up on his threats that he was laughing at him. Just like back in high school. Underwood treated him like a joke then, too. But this wasn't high school. Things were different now.

"Look, you sit there as long as you want and figure things out," Underwood said. "I'm dead tired. I'm going back to sleep."

Merry got up from the chair and approached the bed.

"Come on," Jack said. "Come closer and I'll break your neck."

Merry was so tempted to shoot him, but he had to find out where Lilac was. And he didn't want the neighbors to hear a gunshot if he could help it.

As he got closer, Jack suddenly reached for the nightstand

next to his bed. Merry leapt forward and hit Underwood in the head with the butt of his gun once. Twice.

"*Now* you can sleep awhile," he said.

He opened the drawer of the nightstand. There was a gun in there. Merry closed the drawer again.

Then he made a phone call.

CHAPTER 83

There was blood everywhere.

Francie wasn't going to die from her wounds, but she was in a panic. Ariadne had hurt her just enough. First, she had used the drill to pierce her ear, or rather make the hole that was already there bigger. A *lot* bigger. And then she had taken out a straight razor and severed the ear completely.

She showed it to her, to let her know she wasn't fucking around.

The look in her eyes told Ariadne she got the message and was scared as hell. All the blood didn't hurt. It looked a lot worse than it was.

Francie had been working for the organization for years. She'd known Reynold for years. Her friendship with Ariadne was legitimate; they'd been friends since childhood, but she'd been convinced to use that friendship to spy on Ariadne and report back to her bosses.

Francie was afraid of them. But betrayal was betrayal. Ariadne took it hard, though she didn't show it. Much.

"I did everything I could to protect you," Francie said. "I really love you, you know. I always have. I wanted to tell you the truth so many times. But it was safer this way. I could protect you from the inside. You wouldn't even know."

Ariadne believed that Francie loved her. That Francie really believed, in some twisted way, that she would be able to protect her this way. It was too bad. Their relationship had gone in a completely new direction, and Ariadne was really starting to enjoy it. But there was a *limit* to love.

"I can't forgive you for this," Ariadne said.

"I told you everything," Francie said. "Everything you wanted."

"You should have told me sooner. I shouldn't have had to force you. You should never have agreed to spy on me. If you really loved me, like you said, you shouldn't have gotten involved with them; you shouldn't have kept all these secrets from me.

"All this time, we worked for the same people and I never even knew it. I confided in you. You were the only person I ever trusted. I told you everything. I even told you about Mitch. About killing him."

"Reynold told me before you did," Francie said. "I already knew. You didn't tell me until days later."

"It was painful, for Christ's sake! I had to have time to process it all. But I told you, didn't I? I trusted you!"

"I'm sorry," Francie said. "But I always looked out for you. I always defended you to them."

"Why *wouldn't* you?" Ariadne said. "I never did anything that needed defending. I didn't betray *you*. I never even betrayed the people I worked for. I was always straight with them. What a fool I've been."

She put the gag back in Francie's mouth. Then she got some gauze and medical tape from the bathroom and came back. She sterilized the wound and then covered it up, while Francie squirmed beneath her. It was still bleeding, and would for a while, but the gauze helped.

The phone rang.

Ariadne hesitated. She thought it might be Reynold checking up on her.

After the third ring, the message machine picked it up. She was so tempted to pick up the phone and give Reynold a piece of her mind, but she wasn't ready to talk to him yet. She still wasn't sure what she was going to do with Francie.

There was the sound of the beep, and then someone started to leave a message.

"Ariadne?" a man's voice said. "Are you *there*, Ariadne? I really need to talk to you"

"Merry?" she said, picking up the receiver.

"Yeah," he said. "Ariadne, I need you."

He sounded like he'd been crying.

"Merry, what is it?"

"I didn't want to call. I wanted to respect your privacy. But I was able to track down your new number. I really need your help."

"Sure, Merry. I'll help you. What's wrong?"

"Can you come to where I am? I'll explain everything when you get here. There just isn't much time."

Ariadne looked down at Francie.

"Sure, Merry. I can come over. I'm just wrapping something up here. Give me the address."

He gave it to her, and she wrote it down.

"I'll be there soon. Maybe half an hour?"

"Thank you, Ariadne," he said. "Oh, and bring your bag. I'm gonna need you to help me get some answers out of someone."

"Okay," Ariadne said, finding this last bit of information surprising. This wasn't some tearful reunion. This was *a job*.

"I have to go meet Merry," Ariadne said. "But we're not done talking yet. You'll have to be patient until I get back."

Francie tried to talk beneath the gag, but her words were muffled.

Ariadne went and got some strong wire from the closet and reinforced Francie's restraints.

"Stop struggling," Ariadne said. "Just be thankful you're not dead. When I come back, we'll finish talking, and I'll decide what to do with you."

Ariadne made sure her bonds were secure and tight, then she got ready to go meet Merry.

CHAPTER 84

" So I've been seeing this girl," Merry said. "And we were down in Florida, and she left with another guy."

"Sorry to hear it," Ariadne said.

"I'm sure she left against her will. She hated this guy. She had to have been drugged or something. She and I had just had big fight, and maybe she would have left with him to get back at me, but I don't believe it. And I don't trust anything this guy says. I asked him where she is, and he won't give me a straight answer."

"And you want *me* to make him tell you?"

"It's something you're good at."

"I'm a fucking expert," Ariadne said.

They were standing in the living room of Jack Underwood's house.

"I think he did something to her. I can feel it in my bones. I just don't know what."

"Why is this guy out to get you, anyway?"

"I knew him when I was a kid, in high school. He was one of those bully jock asshole types, you know? He still thinks we're kids, and he wants to make me suffer."

"How did he get into the picture, anyway?"

"It's a long story."

"Give me the condensed version."

"This girl I'm involved with, she makes movies. Porn movies. And the guy does too."

"Why were *you* in Florida?"

"We were making a movie," Merry said.

"You, too?"

"Yeah," Merry said.

"*You* were in a porno movie?"

"Yeah."

"Wow, you sure have been having some fun since we broke up, huh?"

"Look, I'm not in a joking mood," Merry said. "I'm really worried about Lilac."

"Lilac? Is that her name?"

"Look, are you going to help me or not?"

"So you confronted the guy," Ariadne said.

"I broke in here while he was sleeping. I jimmied the lock. I even brought my gun and made sure he saw it. I gave him the third degree. But he kept changing his story. I don't know what to believe."

"What about the gun?" Ariadne asked. "Did you threaten to use it?"

"Yeah," Merry said. "He didn't even flinch."

"See, you should have *made* him flinch. You had a fucking gun."

"I wanted to use it. I really did. But in another way, I felt like a kid in high school again. And I was a cop once. I couldn't just shoot a man in cold blood."

"You should have shot him in the kneecap. That would have made him talk. If he still gave you bullshit, shoot out the other knee."

"I left the force because I didn't want to use a gun again. You know that. I guess I still have issues about it. I thought just showing it to him would be enough. I thought I could intimidate him into talking. But he didn't take me seriously. And I couldn't bring myself to cross that line."

"He probably saw the fear in you. He could tell you wouldn't use the gun."

"All I know is I fucked this all up. I didn't want to call you, but I didn't know what else to do. How else to get answers."

"You want me to make him talk."

"Yeah."

"Okay," Ariadne said. "I'll do it."

"Thanks, Ari."

"Even though things got kind of messy when we got divorced," Ariadne said, "I never hated you, Merry. I want you to know that."

"I never hated you either."

"And this guy sounds like real scumbag. Let's see what he has to say, shall we?"

CHAPTER 85

When Underwood came to, he couldn't move. There was a blindfold over his eyes and a gag in his mouth. And he was naked, tied tightly to a chair.

"He's moving," Merry said.

"So what?" Ariadne said.

Underwood squirmed, but it didn't do him any good. He tried to yell, but all he could do was grunt.

"Knock it off," Ariadne said. She punched him hard in the ribs. He was a big guy, and he worked out, and still he felt the punch. It was like another guy punching him.

He stopped squirming.

"We're going to ask you some questions," Ariadne said. "And you'd better give us the right answers, otherwise you're going to feel some pain. Got it?"

Underwood didn't respond.

"I said 'got it,' asshole?" She slapped the side of his head. "Got it?"

He slowly nodded yes.

"Good. I'm going to take the gag off. If you try to cry out, I'll pull your teeth out, one by one."

Underwood nodded again, very slightly.

Ariadne removed the gag. "Where's Lilac?"

"Fuck you!" Underwood said, and laughed.

Ariadne put the gag back on. Then she took the cattle prod she was holding and zapped his testicles.

Underwood tried to scream, but it was muffled.

"Listen, asshole, let's get this straight from the get-go. We don't have time for bullshit. Just answer the questions, or this is going to get ugly fast."

Underwood clenched his teeth.

She removed the gag again. "Let's get it right this time. Where's Lilac?"

He didn't say a word.

She zapped his balls again.

He convulsed against his will but kept his teeth together.

Ariadne opened her black bag. She put the cattle prod back inside and searched for something worse.

Underwood sat there, tied to a chair. His eyes were covered with a blindfold. His testicles were aflame with agony. He was doubled over as much as he could be, but he made as little noise as possible.

"This is going to take some time," Ariadne said to Merry.

She looked through her toys until she decided on the straight razor.

"You look like you could use a shave," Ariadne said.

They'd taken a small den and removed all the furniture, turning it into a makeshift torture chamber. Ariadne was spattered. Merry stood in the doorway, trying to stay out of the way.

"This is turning out to be a busy night," Ariadne said.

There were multiple, deep cuts on Underwood's body, and strips of his flesh hung from him. There were holes from an electric drill. He had held back as long as he could.

When she started shocking his balls again, he couldn't take it anymore. He'd resisted for more than an hour, but he finally reached his limit.

"Okay," he said.

"What?" Ariadne said harshly.

"I'll tell you."

"It's about time."

"She's in an abandoned building. Fourth and Main. Number twenty-seven."

"Merry," Ariadne said. "Go check it out. I'll stay here. Call and let me know what you find. If our friend here is lying, I'll resume the torture."

"I'm not lying," Underwood said.

"You'd better not be."

In all the activity, a circular, flesh-colored bandage dropped from Underwood's chest. At first, Merry barely noticed, but then he saw the odd-shaped hole there. It was two-pronged and reminded him of a keyhole. Merry took off the necklace Lilac had bought him and slid the key off.

He handed it to Ariadne. "What's this for?" she asked.

He pointed to the strange marking on Underwood. "Use it on him if he's lying."

Ariadne held the key, looking at it oddly, as if she didn't understand what he wanted her to do.

Then he left.

CHAPTER 86

Merry got to the address Underwood gave him. It was a storage facility, and he had the key and the unit number. It was almost eerie the way the place was so quiet, as if the units were mausoleums. Maybe some of them were. He wasn't sure what the place would be like when he drove here, and he expected there to be some kind of security person around, but he didn't have to sign in to wander around the units, and he didn't see anyone around who was in charge.

He found the right storage locker and he took the key out of his pocket, and unlocked the door. He opened it, sliding the door up on its tracks into the ceiling, and found himself in a room stuffed with boxes. He turned on the overhead light.

"Lilac," he called out. "Are you in here?"

There was no reply, but Underwood had sworn he put her there, and Merry was going to search every inch of the place. He started moving boxes around. Some of them were so old their bottoms had rotted through and their contents scattered all over the floor. Books, photographs, random items he couldn't identify; he had no interest in the boxes or what they held, he just wanted them out of his way.

He found a long plastic covering, and tore it open. He immediately regretted it. Inside were the putrefied remains of a body that had been long dead, probably for years. He held his nose and ran out of the unit, trying to breathe again. How long had Underwood been doing horrible things? It looked like he wasn't just some guy trying to torment him by kidnapping Lilac, but that he was something more. A serial killer, probably. This made Merry think of where Underwood had lived in

California. If there was a body here, and he hadn't been here in years, then what secrets was he hiding on the west coast?

It was then that he heard a faint rustling. It was coming from inside the storage unit, and he ran back inside, intent on tracking down where it was coming from. The unit was much longer than he first thought, and toward the back there was another long plastic covering, only this one was *moving*.

He ran to it, kneeling down on the metal floor, and ripped at the plastic. Lilac was inside, naked and bleeding from a hundred small cuts. She was in a state of hysteria, thrashing around as he tore the plastic away. She was making odd grunting noises and breathing loudly, and all he could think to do was grab her and hold her close, trying to subdue her and comfort her at the same time.

He had his ear pressed to her chest, and could hear the rapid percussion of her heart.

She started to calm down and stopped struggling in his grip. She put her arms around him and squeezed him tightly.

"Merry," she said. "Is that really you?"

"Yes it is, Lilac," he told her. "You're safe now."

"Jack said he was going to kill me," she said. "He said he was going to do it slow, and send pieces of me to you in the mail first, and then he gave me something that knocked me out. When I woke up, I was sure I was in some kind of grave."

"You're here with me, and you're safe, and he won't hurt you anymore."

"Did you kill him, Merry?" she asked him, her breathing between words still labored. "Is he dead?"

"Not yet," Merry said.

Merry lifted her and carried her outside the unit. He didn't bother to close the door as he continued walking across the lot, to where his car was.

He got the back door open and slid her inside, but not before he kissed her.

"Are you okay?" he asked.

"I think so," she said.

"Maybe I should take you to the hospital."

"No, Merry," she said. "I'm just scared. I want to go back to your place. I don't want to go anywhere else right now. Can you take me back home?"

"Of course I can," he said. "I can take a better look at you there. Make sure everything's okay."

He stayed like that, holding her, feeling her breath on him, and he kissed her again. Then he climbed back out of the car and got in the driver's seat.

"Welcome back," he said.

CHAPTER 87

"You found her?" Ariadne asked.

"Yeah," Merry said. "In a storage unit, just like he said. He must have drugged her, because she was pretty out of it. She's finally starting to calm down a little now. But she was hysterical when she woke up, when I found her. I don't blame her. She really thought she was going to die."

"Maybe you should take her to the hospital," Ariadne said. "Make sure she's okay."

"I suggested that," he said. "But she insisted I bring her back here and put her in my bed. She's calmer now. Just looks like minor scratches, but I'll look her over more thoroughly. Maybe I'll bring her to the hospital in the morning, either way, just to make sure.

"I found another body there," Merry said. "It looked like it had been there for years. It scared the hell out of me, but at least I knew it couldn't be Lilac. I didn't look to see if there were any more bodies in there. Once I heard Lilac wake up and start thrashing around, she's all I cared about."

"So you think he's been doing this all along," Ariadne asked. "That he's some kind of psychopath?"

"It sure looks that way. I wonder what the police would find if they searched his place in California," Merry said. "Speaking of which, what do you want me to do? Do you want me to call the police or not?"

"Just wait a little longer," Ariadne said. "I know people who can help me clean all this up here. We'll tell the police the whole story, but we'll tell them Underwood got away, maybe he was going back to the west coast. If they find him now, after what I did to him, it will just complicate matters."

"Okay, I'll wait until morning."

"Don't worry, if he killed anyone else, they'll find them. The families will get closure. But I'll deal with Underwood."

"The key," Merry said.

"Yeah, what did you mean by that?" she asked. "Using the key on him?"

"It was something I felt when I saw that mark on him. Something I can't really put into words. My whole life I held onto that stupid key, certain that it would have a use someday. Try it on him, see what happens. If it doesn't do anything, then finish him off your own way."

"It sounds really strange, Merry," Ariadne said. "But I'll do it. I'll take care of things here. You just take care of Lilac."

"Ariadne, thank you for helping me get answers out of him," he said. "Thanks for helping me find Lilac again. I can never repay you."

"I'm just glad she's alive," Ariadne said. "From what you say, there's a good chance he could have killed her before we found her. I'm glad he didn't."

"She said he was going to cut off body parts and send them to me first," Merry said. "The sick bastard. Why did he hate me so much? I was a kid he bullied in high school. Why did he act like I was some kind of threat to him?"

"He's insane," Ariadne said. "He's motives probably wouldn't make sense, even if you knew them."

"I'll talk to you tomorrow," Merry said. "I'm going to go back to Lilac now."

"Okay," Ariadne said, and waited for him to hang up the phone.

She was in Underwood's kitchen and opened the refrigerator. She was hungry and tired and there was a half-empty bottle of wine in there that looked tempting. She considered opening it, celebrating the fact that Merry found Lilac and she was alive, but she decided not to. For all she knew, it could be drugged. He could have used it on his victims.

She couldn't trust *anything* in this place.

Ariadne went back into the room she'd turned into a torture chamber. "Miss me?"

Underwood's head hung to his chest. He said nothing.

"I hear you like to kill women," Ariadne said. "Is that true?"

"I like them better when they're dead," Underwood said. His voice was slurred because she had damaged his jaw. He looked up at her, and she could see something like pride in his eyes.

"And I'll like you better when *you're* dead," she told him.

She took the key Merry had left her, and she moved toward him, where he was still tied to the chair.

"What the fuck are you doing?" he asked.

"Shut up," she said, lifting his chin up and finding the odd indentation in his flesh.

She shoved the key into the weird hole in the middle of Underwood's chest, and somehow it fit. It seemed perfectly shaped to take the key. She found that curious.

She turned the key, hard. A look of anguish came over his face.

It wasn't like turning the key in something mechanical. It didn't feel like that at all. When she turned it, she could feel his flesh separate and bones move as she twisted it. In fact, there was a loud click that resulted from metal scraping against bone.

"What the fuck did you do to me?" he said, his eyes wide.

He began to sob. Tears streamed down his cheeks, mingling with blood. He began to spasm uncontrollably.

It was almost as if he had stopped being able to feel, and the key opened that part of him again. All the years of repressed emotions.

She was probably reading way too much into what was happening. But she had never seen anything like this before.

"I'm sorry," he said, between sobs. "I'm so sorry for everything I did."

He had been so tough during the interrogation session, no matter how painful it got. It had taken a lot to break him. And now he was a sobbing child, begging for forgiveness. Because of this *key*. The same key Merry had been wearing around his neck since before she first met him. This stupid key he insisted on wearing all the time that he'd had since he was a kid.

He was so sure he would find out what it opened someday.

And now she *knew*.

"Forgive me," Underwood pleaded. "Please forgive me."

"Too late," she said. Then she plugged in an electric carving knife she'd gotten from the kitchen and turned it on.

"If I was a priest, I could forgive you, but I'm not." She said. "So rot in hell."

CHAPTER 88

Lilac was sleeping now. It had taken a long time, but he finally calmed her down enough, and the utter exhaustion of everything she had been through washed over her like a wave.

He had examined her body, and didn't see any major injuries, but he was still determined to bring her to the hospital in the morning, and call the police about Underwood. By morning, Ariadne would have had enough time to erase any sign of what they had done.

He heard Lilac talking. She was muttering something in her sleep. He didn't understand it.

He wanted to take her into his arms and hug her close, but he didn't want to wake her up, so he got up and went out to the kitchen, suddenly feeling the urge for some scotch.

Before he could find the bottle, there was a knock at the door. He didn't even think as he went to the door and opened it. He thought maybe it was Ariadne, back already from what she was doing, come to see how Lilac was.

It didn't make any sense, but he was tired and not thinking clearly.

When he opened the door, Jay Finch was standing there. He had a gun.

His face was badly bruised, and he moved with a limp. There was a crazy look in his eyes.

"You thought you could get away with beating me up," Finch said. "But I've got my gun this time."

"Get out of here," Merry said. "Or I'll throw you down the stairs."

"I saw you're lights on. I've been waiting for you. I don't care if you're Harvey's son. You're going to pay for what you did to me."

"Look, I don't have time for your bullshit. It's late, and I have a sick girl here. She needs rest. If you wake her up, I'll beat you up again."

"No you won't," Finch said. "I've got my gun this time."

"You said that already, you stupid fuck."

Finch thrust the gun at him and fired three times.

CHAPTER 89

The gunshots woke Lilac from her sleep. She woke up shivering, certain that she was going to die. It took all her courage to pull herself out of bed and walk out of the bedroom. She kept wanting to turn back and crawl into bed, but she had to see if something bad had happened to Merry.

Maybe Underwood had come back for her, and Merry had shot him to death. She hoped that was it.

But when she got to the living room, Merry was on the floor and he wasn't moving, and there was a crazed man standing there, shouting and waving his gun.

"I beat you," the man was saying. "You thought you beat me, but I beat you."

She knelt down beside Merry and ran her hands over him, but he didn't move. There was so much blood. The murderer didn't even seem to notice she was there.

She pressed her ear to Merry's chest, but didn't hear anything. Lilac was crying as she continued to run her hands over him, until she felt the gun tucked into his waistband. She drew it out, and turned off the safety, as the madman who had shot Merry finally became aware of her.

"You killed him," she said.

"He had it coming," the man said, then, "I don't want to hurt you."

"Then don't," she said.

He seemed confused, like he didn't know anyone else was there, and he didn't know what to do next.

She raised Merry's gun and fired. She kept firing until the gun was empty.

And then she held Merry with all her might, rocking back and forth, until she heard the sirens coming.

CHAPTER 90

Ariadne unlocked her apartment door and went inside. Her work was done, and someone would be at Underwood's house now, to clean the scene and get rid of the man's body. And Merry would be calling the police in the morning.

There would be no sign that she was there.

As soon as she closed the door, she heard the sounds of struggling coming from the bedroom. She walked down the hallway and looked inside. Francie was still tied up in the bed naked, trying to wriggle out of her bonds.

"Now what do I do with you?" she said.

Francie tried to talk around the ball in her mouth, without success. Ariadne considered removing the gag, then went back down the hall to the kitchen. She opened a bottle of wine and poured herself a glass. It had been a long night.

She checked her messages. There was only one she had not listened to before. It was from Reynold.

"Ariadne, I really need to talk to you soon," he said. "We've got another urgent job coming up. Call me back when you can."

"Fuck you," she said to the phone, and finished her glass. She filled it up again and went back to the bedroom.

"I've decided that I am done interrogating people," she said to Francie. "I'm retired."

Francie stared up at her.

"I'm so done with all this," Ariadne said.

She put the glass down and grabbed one of the pillows. She bent down and covered Francie's head with it, pressing down hard. Harder. Until Francie was thrashing beneath her, struggling to stay alive, but unable to get away because she was still tied so tightly.

And then she stopped moving.

Ariadne let go of the pillow and stepped back.

"I'm sorry," she said. "But there's no way I could ever trust you again."

She had her things in order. A passport, new identification, a bag that was already packed. They had been ready for a while now. She wouldn't even wait until morning. She would pick a destination at random and just leave. She had more than enough money in her overseas accounts to live very comfortably.

There was a chance they would track her down. There was *always* that chance. But she didn't care. She didn't want to do this anymore.

She slipped off her clothes. She had taken a shower at Underwood's place, because there had just been too much blood, but she still felt dirty. She would take one more shower, and then she would disappear from this place.

I have to give my friends a call, she thought. *After they finish Underwood's, they can clean this place up, too. Francie will disappear, too.*

She slipped into the shower. No matter how much she washed herself, she just didn't feel clean anymore.

Maybe with a fresh start, it would be different.

ABOUT THE AUTHOR

L.L. Soares is the Bram Stoker Award-winning author of the novel *Life Rage*, which was published by Nightscape Books in the fall of 2012. His other books include the short story collection *In Sickness* (with Laura Cooney), and the novels *Rock 'N' Roll*, *Buried in Blue Clay*, and the one you're holding in your hands.

His fiction has appeared in such magazines as *Cemetery Dance*, *Horror Garage*, *Bare Bone*, *Shroud*, and *Gothic.Net*, as well as the anthologies *The Best of Horrorfind 2*, *Zippered Flesh: Tales of Body Enhancements Gone Bad!* Volumes 1 & 2, and *Traps*.

To keep up on his endeavors, go to www.llsoares.com.

He lives in the Boston area.

Curious about other Crossroad Press books?
Stop by our site:
http://store.crossroadpress.com
We offer quality writing
in digital, audio, and print formats.

Enter the code FIRSTBOOK
to get 20% off your first order from our store!
Stop by today!